Tl

MW00723273

JAKE!
I hope you like it :)
♡u like a bro

KERRI SMITH

THE GAMER

KERRI SMITH

www.bookstandpublishing.com

Published by
Bookstand Publishing
Morgan Hill, CA 95037
3329_2

Copyright © 2011 by Kerri Smith
All rights reserved. No part of this publication may be reproduced or transmitted in any form or by any means, electronic or mechanical, including photocopy, recording, or any information storage and retrieval system, without permission in writing from the copyright owner.

ISBN 978-1-58909-909-8

Printed in the United States of America

CHAPTER 1

He held his breath, terrified of what was to come. His only chance was to run for it now, if he didn't run now, while he was free of his chains, he would have to go through more of the hell he was already being put through. It was his only hope. He felt the cut on his calf rip as he ran, warm, fresh blood oozing down his dirty, bloodstained leg.

"Kal!" the voice echoed.

Kal stopped running, for he had been caught. Torture was going to be worse tonight.

Three Weeks Earlier:

Chloe Johnson put on her hoodie to hide her skin from the bite of the freezing raindrops, her shoe diving into a deep water puddle on the sidewalk.

"That's just great," she said plainly, shaking her foot to shake some of the water out of her drenched shoe.

She ran the rest of the way to school, cutting through one of her friends' yard for a shortcut to get away from the rain faster. When she stepped into the building, she heard her shoes squeak, so she wiped them on the rug, but it was already so wet that it barely made a difference. But, living in Oregon came with rain, so she was used to it by now.

"Wet?" Kal came up beside her.

Chloe shook her head, water flying from her dirty-blonde hair and spraying him.

"Hey!" He laughed as he put up his hand to cover his face.

"Hi Kalvin."

Chloe's smile faded, but a fake one quickly took its place.

Kal's attention was immediately and completely re-focused on his girlfriend, Anna.

Chloe walked around them unnoticed, headed to the bathroom to try to dry off. The school might as well have covered the floors and seats with trash bags to waterproof them, because the roof leaked in most if not every classroom, and it was hardly ever dry this time of year. Getting dry was nearly impossible, and a complete waste of time. But Chloe had plenty of time to waste since Kal decided to go out with Anna.

She dried off with paper towels, ringing out her hair in the sink before she walked out, no longer dripping from her hair or clothes, crashing into what felt to her like a brick wall. A brick wall that almost forced her to the ground.

"Sorry!" Kal apologized, "I was just looking for you," he let go of her arm when he was sure she could stand on her own two feet again, "are you okay?"

"Yeah," she answered, taking a misplaced strand of hair from one side of her face to the other.

"You're still wet, I see." He looked down at a wet splotch on his own shirt.

She shrugged with a smile, "I forgot my umbrella."

"Well anyway, I was gonna ask you if you wanted to come with me and Anna tonight. You could bring Aaron along."

"Aaron *Hale*?" She made a face.

Kal laughed, "Guess not. Maybe Max?"

"No," she answered quickly, without even considering it.

"Alex?"

"Nope."

"Tommy?" His voice had a hint of desperation in it this time.

"Nu-huh." She shook her head.

"Will?"

"No."

"Good grief."

She laughed, "I've got plans," she lied convincingly. Saying: '*I don't want to watch you and Anna make out*' could have been a little harsh.

"Again?" Kal seemed to be annoyed, but he quickly recovered at the sight of Chloe's confused face, "I mean, every time I want to go on a double date, my best friend's busy."

She faked a smile, saying "Maybe next time," as she walked around him and ventured into the gym, sitting down on the empty stairs, looking off into the empty gym. Alone.

"It's kinda vacant in here."

The voice made her jump, but she relaxed when she saw the face, "Aaron, hey."

"What'd Kal do this time?" He sat down next to her, letting his backpack fall to the floor, looking at her with curious eyes.

"He just . . . wanted me to ask you to go on a double date with him and Anna."

Aaron frowned, asking, "Why didn't you?"

Her head snapped up quickly, looking at him.

"I meant, you could go with me and we can try to make him jealous." Aaron added quickly, covering up his last question.

Chloe laughed, "That won't work with Kal."

Aaron shrugged, "You never know. Guys can be pretty confusing."

She looked at him curiously, "Why do you have all the right answers here?"

"I know what it feels like to love someone who is absolutely clueless." He answered.

"I don't *love* Kalvin." She corrected, this lie not sounding as convincing as the lie she told Kal in the hallway.

"Fine, to have *great passion* for someone who's absolutely clueless."

Chloe laughed, shaking her head.

"So whataya say? Double date?"

She looked over at him carefully, studying him. Brown hair, blue eyes, fairly straight teeth, not short (but not as tall as Kal), nice clothes, good cologne . . . "Sure."

He put his thumb up, "I'll go brag to Kal."

She laughed lightly, rolling her eyes, "I'm telling you, it's impossible to make that boy jealous."

"Mission Impossible starts now." He pointed to her and made a popping noise, motioning his hand like a gun that had just shot her, putting his bag on his shoulder with his other hand. Then, he put his hands together in the form of a gun, sneaking secret-agent-like out of the gym.

After the bell rang, Chloe stood up, going to her first class: Chemistry. In Chemistry, they were assigned to work in the lab, something neither Chloe nor Kal was any good at, and of course, they had chosen to be lab partners earlier that year (only because Anna wasn't taking Chemistry that hour). She sat down on the stool and set her backpack on the desk, grabbing onto a strange, clear cylinder device and looking at it under great scrutiny.

"Hey partner," Kal sat down, a cheerful smile on his face, "I hear you're coming with us tonight, after all. Aaron told me, he says he can't wait."

Chloe, once again, smiled fakely, "Yeah. Where are we going, anyway?"

"Just some pizza place up the road. It's new." He poked the cylinder device she was holding, "What's that?"

"I . . . have no idea."

"Miss Johnson, Mr. Jennings, will you quiet down please? We're starting class." The teacher, Mr. Richardson, picked up the bucket of safely goggles, "Mr.

5

Jennings, pass these out to everyone. Miss Johnson," he picked up clipboards, "pass *these* out to every group. And Miss Bryant, pass these out to every group." He pointed to bottles of strange liquid.

The three students got up and began passing everything out; but, in all the commotion, each of them tried to go down the same isle, but from three different directions. It ended in a collision, the mystery liquid spilling all over the three of them.

"This is just *not* my day." Chloe complained, looking down at her shirt.

"What is this stuff?" Kal sounded worried as he did the same.

Mr. Richardson sounded agitated, "It's just salt water. Go to the nurse and get new clothes. Go on, hurry up."

The three of them walked out, glad to get out of the classroom.

"That was crazy." Casey Bryant said quietly, looking up at Kal, then down at Chloe.

"Good thing it was just salt water," Kal commented, looking at his wet shirt before he looked over at Chloe, "Poor you. You've been drenched all morning."

"Like I said, it's not my day."

They all turned into the nurse's office together, and then left as she instructed them to get a key to the laundry room in the basement from the office. Kal went in and got the key, returning quickly, tossing the key up into the air and catching it with one hand.

"Hope the basement's not flooded." Chloe said as Kal lead the way.

When the reached the basement door, Kal unlocked it and pushed it open, looking down at the darkness. They strolled quickly down the steps and looked around, and Kal flicked the light switch, but the lights just flickered on and off, until the room was finally pitch black, totally dark.

"Let's just go back upstairs and find more lights," Kal says rationally.

When the door slammed shut at the top of the stairway, Chloe felt a wave of fear swim through her veins, acting like its own life as it ate up her rational thinking until she imaged a Freddy Krueger character appearing behind her. She closed her eyes, grabbing onto Kal's wet shirt sleeve.

The doorknob jiggled and clicked. They were locked in.

"Kal. . . ." Chloe said, terrified.

"It's okay," Kal assured her.

There was a muffled scream right beside them; Chloe squeezed Kal's arm, and there was a loud sound that could only be described as *thwack*, and then a thud. Kal pulled Chloe close as he reached out to try to find the stair rail; thankfully, his foot hit a step, so he began to venture up them, pulling an eager-to-follow Chloe behind him.

Suddenly, the lights came on, the door hanging wide open. The superintendant was looking in, "What are you two doing down here?"

Kal and Chloe looked around for Casey, "Casey Bryant was just down here with us!" He tried to explain.

"Uh-huh, where'd she go?"

"I don't . . . know." He looked around again, looking at Chloe.

"Come on before i tell your principal what you two were doing."

"We were coming down here to change clothes and—" Chloe was cut off.

"I bet you were, now come on."

They gave up, going quickly up the stairs as Kal tried again, "Please, Casey was down here."

"And she just vanished?"

"It got really dark, and all the lights went off," Chloe desperately tried to explain.

"Yeah, I noticed the lights were off. Get back to class."

Kal and Chloe reluctantly closed their mouths and walked on, just as Anna came out of the bathroom.

"Hey," she said when she saw them.

Chloe came to the realization that she was still holding Kal's arm, and she quickly let go, looking awkwardly down at her shoes, cheeks burning as they turned red.

"Back. To. Class." The superintendant ordered.

"Lakeview High School's Casey Bryant was reported missing earlier this morning," the news reporter said without emotion, "by her worried parents. When the school was asked to comment on the disappearance, the superintendant, James Hitchson, reported that two other students say she had gone down to the school basement with them. But when Mr. Hitchson looked in, he only saw two, Casey Bryant nowhere in sight."

Chloe turned off the TV, talking on her cell phone to Kal, "Bet that superintendant feels great."

Kal agreed, "He should have done something."

"Kal, Casey was gone, he wasn't gonna find anything."

"Where could she have gone?"

"That's the thing," Chloe answered, "the only door into the basement is the one at the top of the stairs."

"There's one inside the laundry room. It leads outside." Kal recalled.

"Really. . . ." Chloe thought, biting her lip.

"Hey, do you need a ride to school? It's raining again." He offered, changing the subject.

"Sure," she couldn't help but smile, biting her lip again, but for a different reason this time.

"Be there in ten."

"Can't wait," *that was a dumb thing to say*, "Bye." She hung up quickly and went out on the porch to wait (not before she looked herself over in the mirror to make sure she looked presentable, of course).

When Kal's blue Ford F150 truck rolled into her driveway, Kal opened the door for her. She ran with her backpack to the truck, hopping in quickly to avoid as much rain as possible.

"See," Kal said, "you barely got wet."

She set her bag down on the floor under her feet, her brain on a different subject, "Kal, I've been thinking. The superintendant searched the basement after school yesterday, so he probably picked up the laundry room key if Casey dropped it. Maybe he has it, but if not, then we know she had to be taken through the laundry room."

"Because whoever took her would've had to know he wouldn't be followed," Kal nodded, "we should talk to Hitchson."

The rest of the drive was quiet, the only sound was of the rain pattering against the roof of the truck. Finally, they pulled up and parked in the school parking lot.

"Thanks for the ride," Chloe thanked, pushing her door open.

"You're welcome. Ha, so much for our double date last night. Maybe tonight?"

"Yeah." She didn't mean to sound so disappointed, "Now let's go inside and see about that key."

"Mr. Hitchson," Chloe approached the superintendant, "We—"

"I'm sorry I didn't believe you, I should have taken you two into consideration." He walked away before anything else could be said.

"That . . . made no sense." Chloe went over his words in her head.

"What didn't?" Kal asked, standing beside her.

She grabbed his forearm and dragged him over to the wall, "Hitchson just said, '*I should have taken you two into consideration*'."

Kal paused for a moment before finally saying, "Pen stuck. Can't connect the dots, can I borrow yours?"

Normally, Chloe would have laughed at something like that, especially said by Kal, but this time she explained, "What if *he* took Casey? He seemed pretty dodgey just now, didn't he?"

"Paranoid much, Chlo? How could he have taken her?"

"Most bad guys don't exactly work alone anymore. It's the only way they can stay out of jail, right?" She whispered, ignoring his first question.

"Nice theory, Miss Johnson," Hitchson was standing only a few feet behind Kal, he had been hiding there so she couldn't see him, "an inside job is the most suspected. And I understand your theory, it's very sensible." He stepped towards them, putting each hand on one of their shoulders. "But I really don't appreciate the accusations, Miss Johnson. You should take this quest you've set yourself on into deep consideration before you venture further into extremely uncharted territory."

"You mean the territory of *investigation*, right?" Chloe said smartly.

Hitchson grinned, "That is exactly what I mean." He walked away again, for real this time.

Chloe and Kal's eyes met, and suddenly they were on the same page. "We should go downstairs," he whispered, "after school, meet me at that old swing set we used to play on when we were kids."

"That brings back awful memories." She laughed.

"Braces and pigtail memories?" He teased, smiling.

"Shut up mister overalls and bowl-cut hair."

He chuckled, shaking his head, "Touché." He waved as he backed up, turning around and walking away with his backpack on his shoulder.

She watched him go and she wondered what all went on in his head. Then, she realized she's never really understand, because the male and female species would never understand each other, they were only meant to communicate on somewhat of an understanding and tolerant level. As Kal disappeared out of sight, Chloe's eyes seemed to just wander until they stopped on the office door. Then, she looked through the glass, seeing the office was completely empty.

She glanced around and walked un-noticed into the office, sneaking into a back room, where there were a million keys hanging on the wall, all labeled something different. There were a few with spare keys, and she noticed only one key was hanging that was labeled "Laundry", so she grabbed it.

After school, Chloe was the first to be on the playground outside. It all used to be so much bigger than it was now; after all, now that she was taller and older, it all seemed so small and boring. She sat down in the small swing, remembering the one memory that wasn't so bad about elementary school. . . .

The recess bell rang, all of the kids ran out to play. The older kids, the kids in 6th, 7th, and 8th grade, usually played basketball or swung on the swings. Chloe, as usual, was on the swings as Kal ran up to get a roll-away basketball. She stopped it with her foot and picked it up, handing it to him.

"Thanks, Chloe." He said.

"Sure," she replied with a smile.

"Aww," Alex Robertson, the hot-shot bully who was so much older and bigger than everyone else because he flunked two years teased, "Kal's got a girlfriend."

"Not only are you extremely annoying, you're also immature." Chloe commented.

"We're friends," Kal agreed, "have been since Kindergarten, which you'd know nothing about."

"So grow up," Chloe added.

"You're telling me to grow up?" He spat, "You're the one who cried for hours after your stupid daddy left."

Kal looked at Chloe's pained face, then stepped toward Alex, warning, "Don't talk to her about that"

"Oooh," Alex pretended to shiver, then he looked around Kal to Chloe, "After all the things your dad did to you—"

Alex didn't get to finish because Kal hauled out and punched Alex in the face.

"Kal!" Chloe was surprised, but she quickly grabbed Kal's arm.

Alex got up from the ground, but with his horrible aim and injured eye, he punched Chloe in the face, instead of Kal. Immediately, Kal tackled him, but that was all Chloe remembered until she opened her eyes in the nurse's office, with Kal sitting next to her.

"Hey." He said quietly.

"Ow." She touched her forehead.

"Don't," He grabbed her hand, "it just stopped bleeding. He had a rock."

She looked up at the scrapes on his face: one on his chin and the other on his nose, close to his eye. "Are you okay?"

"Psh, yeah." He let go of her hand and looked her in the eye.

"Thanks for stickin' up for me."

He nodded, "Couldn't let him. . . ." He decided to drop the subject.

She grinned and touched the scrapes on his nose, "Well. Thank you."

He smiled, "I'll always be here to be your bodyguard, Chloe Johnson."

"You better be."

"Chloe," Kal came up beside her, taking her out of the memory, "Sorry," he said after she jumped, "What are you thinking about? How long have you been waiting?"

"Not long." She only answered the last question, avoiding the first one.

He got behind her and gave her a small push, so she grabbed onto the chains, picking up her feet.

"We should go to the basement, I have the key," she told him reluctantly, not wanting to leave.

"We're waiting for Anna first."

She put her feet down, stopping the swing, replying bitterly, "Anna's coming?" If it were a movie, she would have heard the soft music come to an abrupt, screeching halt. "You *told* her?"

Kal backed up a step, "I didn't think you'd mind."

"Kal. The more people who know about me and you checking all the stuff out, the worse it is for us." She was out of the swing, only a couple feet away from him, "We can't get caught."

"Anna understands." He defended his precious girlfriend.

"I'm sure she will." Chloe grabbed her jacket and started walking away, heading towards the school, passing Anna on her way in.

"Hey," Anna said, "I was just coming to meet you and Kalvin."

"Go ahead, he's waiting for you." Chloe brushed past her.

"What's wrong?"

She didn't answer, she just kept walking, telling herself that was mad at Kal because he told *someone*, not because he told *Anna*. She opened the basement door and shut it behind her, the room was as dark as the fur on a black cat. Her anger over-powered her fear, and she walked right down the stairs, flipping on the light switch. It came on with ease this time, just like she expected it to. It must have been messed with by whoever it was that kidnapped Casey.

"What's going on with Chloe?" Anna asked Kal.

Kal sat down on the ground, "Honestly, I'm not sure. She's so hard to understand sometimes."

"You've known her since forever." Anna hid the jealousy in her voice.

"We should go help her."

"Kalvin, I don't think she wants our help."

He looked at her, "Maybe you're right."

She nodded, "I am. Meet me at my house tonight?" She bit her lip, "My parents are at a fancy dinner with dad's boss."

"Uh, sure. Later, there's some stuff I have to get done first." He swallowed, hoping she wouldn't ask.

"Okay, sure." She kissed him, "See you later."

"Bye," he watched her go before he wiped the lip gloss from his mouth, jogging toward the school.

Chloe opened the laundry room door, slipping the key back into her pocket. She had never been in the laundry room before, so she looked around. There were two washing machines and two dryers against the wall to her right. There was a narrow hallway continuing into the room, but it ended soon, turning right. She closed the laundry room door and started down the uncharted territory; suddenly, the shadow of a man slid across the floor, making her jump and hide against the wall. She saw the feet walk towards her, so she quickly looked up at the face.

"Miss Johnson."

"Mr. Hitchson," her voice quivered.

"I told you to stop." He forcefully pushed a rag to her mouth, and she struggled, but the horrible scented fluids on the rag made her go limp. Within seconds, everything was dark for her.

Kerri Smith

CHAPTER 2

Chloe opened her eyes.

"Hey," Kal said, kneeling down by her.

They were still in the laundry room, Chloe noticed as she looked around, "Kal? When did you? . . . How?" Her mind was dazed.

He helped her sit up, but made her lean against the wall as he explained, "I sent Anna home and came in to help you. And to apologize," he added, quickly moving on, "Hitchson was trying to drag you out."

She saw the blood running out of his busted lip, and a bruise already forming on his eyebrow, she raised her own eyebrows as she asked, "So what happened?"

"I came at him, so he pulled a knife," he went on quickly at the horrified look on Chloe's face, "but he didn't get a chance to use it because I grabbed this belt and hit him with the buckle." He finished proudly.

She looked at him, eyebrows still raised.

"He dropped the knife and we . . . went into a little fight thing."

"A little fight thing?" She used her thumb to wipe blood off of his lip and chin, "You're bleeding like crazy."

"Does that mean you aren't mad at me anymore?" He took her hand and helped her stand up.

"Why'd you send Anna home?" She questioned curiously.

"Doesn't matter," Kal shrugged.

"It does to me, Kal." *Oh gosh, I can't believe I just said that*, "I mean, if you absolutely want a third person to this little investigation party, whatever." She brushed off her pants, "But I personally don't think Anna's. . . ."

"Bold enough?" Kal asked, as if he agreed.

"Mhm. Man, my head hurts." She put her fingers to her temple, then she looked at the knife that was on the floor, "So, Hitchson just . . . left?"

"Yeah. It was weird." He touched his swelling eyebrow, "We were swinging and knocking the hell out of each other, then he pushed me into the wall and ran out."

"Just like that?"

Kal made a face, "Well . . . he might have possibly locked us in. And about the working with a partner thing, I think he is because the other door was locking at the same time."

"Oh," Chloe said plainly.

"Come on," he walked toward the door that lead to outside as Chloe got up and grabbed the knife, walking toward the other door, the one leading into the basement.

They both tried opening the doors at the same time, and both were definitely locked. "Now what?" Kal asked, looking around.

Chloe looked at the walls, seeing they were built just like the walls of the basement. She looked at the ceiling, seeing the easy access tiles so you could get into the ceiling to work (usually on water damage), "We go up there." She pointed.

"Well don't you have a key?"

"It's a one side lock."

"Okay, the ceiling it is." He agreed, climbing on top of a washing machine and carefully stretching up to try to touch one of the tiles on the ceiling, "I . . ." he tried stretching farther, "I can't . . ." his foot slipped and he fell off of the washing machine, catching himself partially.

Chloe's tight grip on his shirt preventing his head colliding with the floor. He shakily stood up, looking at the rip at the neck of his shirt. He was breathing hard, his heart slowing back to its normal rate.

"Thanks," he finally said, "Nice reflexes."

She nodded, "Are you okay?"

"I'm still in one piece, as far as I know." He looked down at his chest and patted it, looking back up at the ceiling tiles, "If you sit on my shoulders, we can get it."

She looked at him awkwardly, recovering with, "But if you slip again, we're both dead."

"True," he nodded, "but maybe if we scoot the washing machine out a little...."

"Fine." She agreed, seeing no other option.

They worked together to scoot the washing machine as far out as they wanted it, then Kal climbed on, holding out his hand to help her up. Now, they were forced to stand close, the surface of the washing machine not giving them much room. When Chloe tried to step away, the heel of her shoe slipped and Kal caught her before she went over the edge. He was holding onto her elbows, his knee touching the side of her thigh.

Like this helped the awkwardness Chloe was trying to escape.

But, of course, it wasn't awkward for Kal. If it was, he didn't show it "Okay," he made sure she could stand, "now get on my back and sit on my shoulders."

"Oh, okay." She said sarcastically, looking at him.

He got on his knees slowly, steadying himself.

"This isn't at all safe, Kal." She warned him, putting her hands on his shoulders.

"Just try."

She felt his muscles in his shoulders tighten as he braced himself, sturdying himself so he wouldn't fall when she put her weight on him. She tried not to get distracted by this as she lifted her leg to put over his shoulder.

"Ready?" She asked him.

"Yeah."

She jumped slightly, both feet over his shoulders. They sat there paused for a little while, adjusting to the weight difference, balancing out on their surface (which seemed to be smaller now that it was harder to balance). Kal finally began to stand, Chloe shutting her eyes, holding on to the sides of Kal's neck.

When they stood, Kal turned a little, causing Chloe's head to crash into the light bulb, and it shattered as Chloe made a noise that was between "aah", "ugh", and "ow" as they both fell to the floor. Kal fell first, making Chloe fall onto the edge of the washing machine, he hit the floor, landing on his back with a loud thud as Chloe slid off, landing on top of him.

And now the lights were off, which didn't help matters.

But Chloe was in too much pain to deal with the awkward moments. She rolled off of him, feeling warm blood seep out of the back of her head from the light bulb. Kal sat up, dizzy because the wind was literally just knocked out of him.

"What happened?" He asked, "I heard glass." He looked up and saw the shattered bulb through the darkness, then he looked at Chloe, "Are you okay?"

She touched the back of her head, looking at the blood on her fingertips.

"I'm sorry!" He quickly hunched over her.

"You apologize too much," she complained, sitting up.

There was a small pause as Chloe touched at the cut on her head, but Kal broke the silence with a little bit of his humor, "Looks like our double date's canceled again."

"Yep."

He looked at her, squinting, "You did this on purpose, didn't you?" He joked.

"It's my master plan to avoid ever spending any more after school time with you." She grinned mysteriously, the grin followed by another short pause, causing her to change the subject back to seriousness, "At least we know for sure Hitchson's doin' it."

"So optimistic." He shook his head, "So what's plan C?"

"Dig through the floor." She answered without hesitation.

He looked down at the floor, swallowing.

"Kidding," she assured him.

He nodded, "Oh, good."

She laughed a little, more concerned about the pain in her head. She touched it again, trying to keep her face straight, although she wasn't doing the best job.

"Chlo, are you sure you're okay?"

"Yeah," she quickly retracted her hand from her head, fresh blood on it.

"Let me look," he insisted, scooting over to her. He got behind her, looking at her bloody hair, "Oh, crap."

"You can't say *let me look* followed by *oh crap* when you're looking at the back of my cut head, Kal." She found it weird that she didn't even wince as Kal parted her hair away, gently touching her scalp next to the two cuts.

"There's still glass in one."

"Lovely," she replied.

"It doesn't look too deep...." He trailed off, studying her bloody hair.

"Pull it out."

He froze.

"What?" She turned to look at him.

"You want me to pull glass out of your head?" He said it like it was some dangerous law he was breaking.

"You said yourself, it's not that deep," she reminded him slowly.

"Yeah, but if I'm wrong—"

"Kal, it hurts like hell, will you just try?" Her voice was desperate.

He agreed, "Okay, okay."

Chloe sat there calmly, with her eyes closed. It didn't even hurt that much as he slid the glass out of her head, and after he set that glass on the floor, he touched her bleeding cut. It stung a little, but she let him; after all, it hurt a lot less now that the glass was out.

There was a noise, like the sound of a door swinging shut, it came from the basement. Was someone coming in? Or, the more important question, was this person friendly, or were they just coming to collect what they have trapped? Kal and Chloe stood up in unison, looking at the door that leads to the basement as the doorknob jiggled loudly. Whoever it was on the other side, they obviously didn't have a key. Then, the doorknob on the other door jiggled, but it began to open, the other door opening soon after.

Kal grabbed Chloe and pulled her into a spot in between the wall and the dryer, where they crouched down to hide, his arm around her to keep her out of sight. The janitor came in from the basement, jingling all of his spare keys in his hands as Hitchson came in from outside, the key he stole from Casey Bryant in his hand.

"Mr. Hitchson," the janitor said, "what happened to the washer?"

Hitchson looked around for Chloe and Kal, a worried look on his face. Pulling a gun from his back pocket, he didn't hesitate to pull the trigger on the shocked janitor. Chloe wanted to scream at the sound of the gun and at the sight of the janitor's chest pierced with a bullet, at the sight of the blood leaking down his chest as he fell to his knees, the gun smoking; thankfully, Kal knew her too well, so he covered her mouth with his hand, holding her tightly. After Hitchson looked around to make sure he was still alone, he looked up at the tiles on the ceiling, his gun returning to his back pocket. He climbed up onto the washing machine swiftly, reaching up for the tiles.

Kal stood up slowly, Chloe's mouth still covered; she was still in his arms. He looked her in the eye, then looked at the door that lead to outside, the one that Hitchson had come in through, then he moved his hand away from her mouth slowly. Hitchson lifted up the tile and peeked in, his eyes scanning the darkness for any sign of Kal or Chloe, but there was nothing. He took his head out from the attic, looking at the smashed light bulb, then at the blood spots on the floor, jumping down from the washing machine. As he looked behind the wall, behind the washing machine, and the little place that was in between the wall and the dryer; a perfect place to hide; but, there was nothing.

Kal and Chloe were running as fast as they could, hand in hand to make sure they stayed with each other, to make sure neither (Chloe, mainly) got left behind. They both knew where they were going: Kal's house, it was closest, and they needed to get somewhere safe *now*. They burst through the door, scaring Kal's father.

"Sorry Dad," Kal said as he looked out of the window cautiously.

"What the hell's goin' on?" his father asked, weary.

"Nothin'," Kal said, glancing at Chloe, "we're just...."

"Playing a game," Chloe finished.

"Yeah," Kal agreed.

"Hide and seek."

"Okay...." He went back to watching his television show, no longer worried.

Kal hurried to the stairs, going up them to his room as Chloe awkwardly waiting downstairs, wishing she knew what his sudden idea was since he took off without warning; without a *follow me* or a *stay here, Chloe.* He came back down with his cell phone in his hands, dialing a number and putting it to his ear.

"Hey, Anna?"

Oh.

"Hey," he talked fast, "I'm sorry, babe, but I can't make it tonight." *Pause,* "We're canceling the double date, too." *Short pause,* "Because. Aaron has other plans," he lied. "I still can't come over tonight." *Short pause,* "I'm hanging out with Chloe, okay? Just not tonight." *Very long pause,* "Anna, there's nothing to be jealous about."

Gee, thanks.

Kal's father looked at Chloe, but she pretended not to see him as she looked off at a wall that suddenly became very interesting.

Meanwhile, Kal went on, "We just have some lab stuff to do." *Pause,* "Yes, it'll take all night." *Pause,* "I'll see you tomorrow." He hung up, complaining, "Jeez," as he threw his phone onto the couch, "that was…" he trailed off, looking at his father, "Hey Dad, me and Chloe are gonna go upstairs for a little while."

Chloe started up the stairs, eager to get out of the awkward stare his dad was giving her because of the phone call, Kal on her heels.

"Kal," his father called, stopping him.

They both froze on the spot, looking down at him.

"Let me talk to you a minute."

Kal looked at Chloe and nodded once, telling her to go upstairs without him, then he went back down as Chloe gradually progressed her speed, starting very slow, until she was finally behind the wall to eavesdrop, although she wished she hadn't afterwards.

"There are some . . . certain things in the left corner of the medicine cabinet in the bathroom. I want you to . . . use them."

Kal looked confused.

His father elaborated, "If you're going to . . . you know . . . with more than one girl, especially, you have to…."

"Dad!" Kal said quickly, shaking his head.

"Even though, I must say, I like Chloe a lot more than I like Anna, but it's still wrong to cheat—."

"Really?"

"Just please," he urged after a short pause, "use . . . one of them things."

Kal closed his eyes and ran his fingers through his hair, laughing slightly to himself as he started back up the stairs. Chloe quickly went into his room so he didn't know she was eavesdropping; although, she couldn't look at the room in the same way anymore. And worse, she couldn't get certain images out of her mind.

Kal came in, still slightly laughing as he shut the door, "My dad. Has issues. He really needs to work through them."

Uh, yeah. She thought, looking at him.

"So," he said, voice back to serious-mode, "Which do you wanna do first? Go to the police and rat Hitchson out, or, stay here and put together a bunch of our evidence and stuff to blackmail him for all his money?"

Chloe, still on the sex subject, asked, "Your Dad's okay with me and you being up here alone?" She enjoyed this slightly, laughing on the inside.

He hesitated, thinking of a good way to answer, "Yeah, he's fine with it."

Sure, go with that. The voice in her head strained with laughter, but her actual voice was calm and collected, "We should stay here and collect evidence. Not to blackmail him, but to build a case on him so the police'll believe us when we rat him out." She sat down at his computer, moving his mouse to stop the screen saver. Feeling a slap in the face as she laid her eyes on his wallpaper: a picture of him and Anna, so she quickly got on the internet, typing in: *news about school kidnapping.* A few came up, but only one about their high school, so she clicked on it and she and Kal both leaned forward closer to the computer screen as a security tape of the basement showed, in night vision, Chloe clutching Kal's arm as a masked man hit Casey over the head with a gun, dragging her out of sight and toward the laundry room. The scene stopped, then restarted at the beginning again.

"They don't think it's Hitchson at all." Kal stated.

Chloe looked up at him, their faces only inches apart. He looked down at her.

"What the hell?" Anna was standing in the doorway, arms crossed, looking from Kal to Chloe.

"Anna, I told you," Kal stood up, "we're—"

"Not doing chemistry," She butted in, glaring at an embarrassed Chloe.

"We're working on something important." He argued,

"Don't get all stressed out, Anna, you'll get a pimple and ruin that pretty little face of yours," Chloe stood up, "Don't worry either, I'm leaving."

"Chloe," Kal tried, looking at her.

"Kal," she looked at him desperately, trying to telepathically communicate with him. Luckily, they had been best friends long enough, they had that best friend telepathy. "You should hang out with your girlfriend, I'll see you later."

Translation: Come over later.

"Okay, sure. Thanks Chlo."

Translation: No thanks, I'll be over as soon as I possibly can!

Kerri Smith

CHAPTER 3

Chloe walked into the house, avoiding her mother's gaze.

"Where've you been?"

"I was at Kal's." She tried going around her mother.

"This whole time?" She blocked Chloe's way, stepping in front of her.

"No, we got held after school," she answered truthfully, then we were working on a project at his house." She pushed past her mother, done talking.

"Your father called."

She froze in her tracks, barely able to talk, mouth suddenly dry, "He did?" She worked hard to make her dry throat swallow.

"He asked to see you."

She turned around to face her mother, "And you told him . . . what, exactly?"

"I told him it was your decision. His number's on the fridge." She finished her sentence quietly, dismissing herself from the conversation by walking quickly into the kitchen.

Chloe went into her bedroom, shutting the door absentmindedly. She laid down, thinking; then, not long after she laid down, she dozed off. Her dream was just a memory, it was exactly what had happened, her brain just wanted her to relive it....

She came home from school one day, in the 7th grade, going into the house. Her father was pushing her mother into the wall, hand on her neck; then, he looked at Chloe, throwing his wife down onto the floor.

"You knew about this!" He accused.

Before she had time to think, he back-handed her, and she dropped her back and was forced into the wall. He grabbed her hair and pulled it, making her face look up at him.

"You knew she was gonna leave me, didn't you?" He pulled her hair harder, face closer to hers, "Didn't you!?"

"No," she croaked, grabbing onto his arm to try to push him off.

"Don't touch me," he hit her again.

Her mother got up and ran for the door, trying to get outside, where she left her cell phone. She ran out the door, but Chloe's father ran out after her.

He yelled, "I'm not gonna sit back and let you leave me!"

Half of the neighborhood was forming a crowd, hearing the commotion. Kal was there, Chloe noticed, and Anna, the bully Alex, she knew everyone that was standing around.

Her father pulled a gun, but Chloe jumped on him from behind before he could use it on her mother. He threw her off of him and she crashed onto the back of a parked car that was on the curb. Three people tried to hold Kal back, but he pushed past them as Chloe's father began to hit her with the gun; over and over again he swung, he swung harder and harder each time. Kal, who was only barely half of her father's size, pushed him, resulting in the bloody gun being aimed at his face.

"I'll shoot you, kid."

The police sirens were faint, but they were getting stronger. Her father snapped into action, putting the gun into his jacket pocket, shoving some of the scared crowd away and running away quickly.

Kal turned to Chloe, who was crying and holding her bloody face in her hands as she laid on the ground. He sat down and pulled her into his arms, rocking her back and forth, comforting her as the sirens grew constantly louder.

"You're fine, you're gonna be fine." There was already blood all over him, most of it streaming from all of the deepest cuts, the ones on her forehead and above her temple, "It's okay, you're okay. He's gone."

She had her fists clenched in pain, holding his shirt as tightly as she could, all she wanted was for the pain to stop. That's all she wanted.

Chloe opened her eyes, seeing Kal shutting her bedroom door softly. She looked at the clock, "Kal, it's almost midnight."

"Sorry," he whispered, "she wanted to watch a movie. Did I wake you up?"

"How'd you sneak in without my Mom seeing?" She sat up tiredly.

"She was asleep on the couch, bed head." He sat down on her bed next to her, looking at her messy hair.

As she brushed her fingers through her hair, fixing it as good as possible, she touched the scar on her head. The one right above her temple. It wasn't very noticeable with her hair just right, but she could swear some people always stare. Like her mother; the scars were all her mother saw when she looked at her.

"What's wrong?"

He always read her like a book. "My . . . Dad called."

Kal looked angry, "Why?"

Chloe shrugged, "He wants to see me."

He clenched his jaw tightly, "Are you . . . gonna do it?"

She looked him in the eyes, "He's my Dad, Kal. He's on probation, so he's not gonna do anything stupid."

"But you don't know that, Chloe." He argued, "You have no idea how . . . how mangled you looked. He did that to you, Chlo." He touched the scar on her forehead, "He almost killed you. He may be your father, but he's not your dad."

Tears formed in her eyes as Kal's reality check sunk in, "You're right," she blinked a few times, stopping the tears.

He hugged her, his arms reaching entirely around her, "I just don't think it'd be safe."

She nodded, her head resting on his chest, "I know."

He kissed the top of her head and released her from the hug, looking at her from eye to eye, not breaking his stare.

"Anyway," she said, looking away, wanting to change the subject.

"Yeah," he agreed, "anyway."

"We should get to work on the thing." She felt light headed, still feeling his touch on her skin.

"The thing." He agreed again.

"That's getting slightly annoying."

"Annoying," he nodded.

She laughed, shaking her head and pushing him softly. He was always so good at making her feel better. He knew all the right things to say, even if it meant saying nothing at all. He always made her laugh.

The next day, Chloe worried almost all day; she didn't see Kal until lunch.

"Hey," he popped up out of nowhere again besides her, causing her to push her quarter into the vending machine a little harder than intended.

"Holy crap, Kal."

"Sorry," he laughed lightly, looking at her head, pushing a few strands of hair aside to see the cuts, "I see your light bulb accident has scabbed. Bet that sucked when you brushed your hair."

"Yep," she pressed two buttons, watching the greed Gatorade slide into the slot and fall with some thuds.

Kal took it out for her, opening it and taking a few gulps.

"Uh, hello!" She tried to steal it back from him.

He held it up out of her reach, "One more drink."

She glared at him, squinting slightly as he slowly took another drink before handing it to her.

"You look tired," she commented.

"I didn't go home last night," he said, like it was normal.

"Why not?" She asked, concerned, taking a drink of her Gatorade and screwing the lid back on.

"My Dad would've thought . . . let's just say I spent the night with Adam."

"Oh. Well," she asked, "after school—"

"Hey, Kalvin!" Anna called, clutching his shirt, pushing a huge gap in between him and Chloe,

Chloe's mouth pulled back slightly in disgust at the overpowering, strong scent of way too many sprays of perfume. She stepped back and, not knowing what else to do, she took a drink of her half-gone green Gatorade.

"Wanna come over again tonight?" Anna suggested, "Or we could always go to your house. I think your Dad's words were something like: *you know I don't like talkin' 'bout this kinda stuff, but make sure you use one of them things*, weren't those his words?"

Chloe, in mid swallow, sprayed green Gatorade everywhere. She couldn't tell if she was laughing because it was a *one of them things* talk, or if it was because it was Kal's Dad, or if she was angry and shocked. Maybe it was all three. Anna laughed at her mess, but her snicker quickly dissolved when Kal grabbed the bottle from Chloe.

"I think you've had enough," he said before finishing it off, shooting it like a basketball into the nearest trashcan.

Chloe laughed a little as she looked back at Kal, following an annoyed teacher to get a mop, "It's in there," they told, pointing vaguely and walking away, obviously having something better to do.

She walked into the dark storage room, the dim lights hurting her eyes. She opened the door to the back, daylight eliminating the room quickly; then, she looked around for the mop, seeing the bucket in the corner as the bell rang to start class.

"Hi, Chloe."

She froze. Without control, her hands began to shake as she asked quietly, "Dad?"

"You're so big now."

She turned around, looking at him, "You can't be here." With that she grabbed the bucket and mop and walked toward the doorway to go back into the hallway, back where there were other people; although, a crowd didn't stop him last time, did it?

"Chlo, I just wanna talk to you," he grabbed her arm.

"*Don't*," she gritted her teeth, "Don't touch me," her tone was warning enough.

He backed away, hands in surrender, "I'm sorry, I'm sorry."

"It's too late for sorrys, *Dad*," she spoke his name with a bitter voice, turning to walk away from him, Kal's words echoing in her head.

"He almost ended your life…he may be your father, but he's not your Dad."

"Chlo, wait." He pleaded.

"Goodbye. Have a nice life," she ended the conversation, walking out.

First hour: chemistry. Chloe waited for Kal, but he never came; so, worrying intensely, she tried her hardest to pay attention and focus on her work. Finally, with 10 minutes left of class, Kal came in, a note for the teacher in his hand. He sat down with a blank look on his face, which worried Chloe even more.

"You okay?" She was going to tell him about her little encounter with her father, but he seemed to be really upset.

He looked at her, surprised, "You didn't hear?"

"Hear what?"

"About Hitchson…. What happened after you left…?"

Chloe figured she must have been too distracted by her father to notice anything unusual, "Uh…no."

He looked at her, hesitated, then explained in a low whisper, "After you left to get a mop, Hitchson asked me and Anna to go into his office."

Her eyebrows creased downward, her worrying was steadily increasing into what might possibly lead to some sort of an anxiety attack of some sort.

"I couldn't say no. I mean, who's everyone here gonna believe, me or him?"

Now her eyebrows rose in disbelief, "You went in there?"

He nodded plainly, looking her in the eyes.

She waited, and when she figured out he wasn't elaborating, she urged him to, "So what happened?"

He hit me out of the way and grabbed   Anna.   He said something about easy bait. And he took her."

She sat in disbelief for the longest time before she could force anything out of her mouth, "Other people saw?"

He shook his head.

"Now people still don't know it's Hitchson, that's great." But the sad look at Kal's face wasn't a good thing. Chloe's turn to comfort: "That means her parents'll report it and the cops will be on it soon. And plus, Hitchson needs Anna, she's bait for us."

"Us?"

She answered, "He must know by now that wherever you go, I'll follow."

He nodded, then leaned his head on his shoulder. She didn't mean to smile, it just happened, and she leaned her head onto the top of his, like a mini-hug, deciding that her bad news could wait.

Anna could only see the front of a house as she was being dragged by her feet, the sidewalk burning her back.

The house was dark, windows were covered, and the yard was naked, no green in sight. She was thrown into a room, seeing the dirt-smeared face of Casey Bryant.

2 weeks later:

Chloe hung up her cell phone, going quickly down the stairs, her brain almost moving too fast for her feet to handle.

"Where are you going?" Her mother asked.

"I have to go meet Kal."

"No. Not today." She said plainly, as if there would be no arguments.

"It's Saturday night." Chloe protested.

Her mother shot back, "You've been going over there way too much."

"His girlfriend's been kidnapped for over two weeks. I'm not gonna leave him alone to cry."

"Exactly, there's a kidnapper out there, I don't want you leaving the house this late. You can hate me all you want, but you're still not leaving. You may think I'm the meanest person in the world, but that's who mothers are supposed to be. It's for your own protection."

Chloe looked at her mother for a moment, brain swimming with what she was going to do next. Then, she opened the front door and walked out, her mother's yells completely blocked out by the loud sound of silence in her brain. She ran the few blocks to Kal's house; but, when she got there, her eyes widened and her mouth dropped open, shock and dread swimming through her veins, up and down her body.

Orange flames licked the roof, eating away the doors, blackening the windows. The fire looked like it had just been set, probably with the help of gasoline all over the house, because she would have seen the smoke from her house, definitely. The truck that was screeching away caught her attention, and she quickly looked at the license plate, quickly taking out her cell phone and snapping as many pictures as she could before quickly dialing Kal's number, hands shaking violently.

The phone didn't even ring.

"Dammit!" She fumbled with the buttons of the phone, dialing 911, staring at the house as the evil heat touched her face, matching the burning in her eyes.

Kal peeked out of the back of the truck he was forced into, seeing his house burning. He saw Chloe! "Chloe!" He yelled through the cloth in his mouth. She couldn't hear him, so he rested his head against the window helplessly, riding obediently with his hands tied together, watching the outside world carefully to try to memorize where he was going and how to get there.

Finally, the truck stopped and his door opened, making him fall out of the truck because he was leaning on it. He was being dragged by his tied-together wrists, all the way into the house. All he could see was the front of the house, the dirt trail was the only bald part of the yard, beautiful green grass all around.

Chloe sat in her bed, her tears on hold, waiting for the next wave of emotion to come through. Kal was dead; they found a body burned in the house, trapped under the fallen shelf, another body on the couch. It was all her fault; after all, she was the one who forced him into the investigation and he got killed for it. She wasn't going to stop until she got her revenge.

Feeling the next set wave of emotion slowly creeping up on her, she grabbed the box of tissues, closing her moist eyes.

CHAPTER 4

At school Monday morning, Chloe sat alone in the gym, trying to get a grip on her roller-coaster of emotions. It was like one second she was fine, but the next, Kal's face invaded her mind and she would completely break down. She even had to stop the car a couple of times on the way to school, silent tears streaming down her face out of her closed eyes. She would sometimes yell angrily and hit the dash or a part of the steering wheel before she would wipe away her tears and begin to drive again. The worst part was passing Kal's house on the way. The burned down house making it seem so cold, so empty. So...dead.

As she sat in the gym, she saw Aaron and his friends peek in at her from afar for a while before they walked away. Miserably, she still sat all alone, still expecting Kal to walk in and smile. She would kill to see that one last time. Hell, she would even take Kal with Anna if that was what it took. She just wanted him back, that was all.

She needed him.

Chloe looked over; instantly, her heart stopped as her eyes saw Hitchson standing in the office. How!? She jumped up, glaring at him, feeling an intense hatred that she had never felt before. He looked at her, smiling.

Coach Walden walked into the gym, so Chloe asked him demandingly, "Why is Hitchson here? He killed—"

"He's been cleared of all charges. He was in custody when Kal's house...." After he paused, he walked away awkwardly, not knowing what else to do.

She let a few more tears come out before she looked at Hitchson again. Time for revenge: She went into Hitchon's office without hesitation, shutting the door loudly.

"Hello, Miss Johnson."

"Why'd you kill him?" She couldn't even say his name, voice shaking.

"I didn't. And I've had enough of your false accusations." He stood up, body language speaking threat.

"You gonna kill me, too?" Her eyes watered again, "Put me under a shelf and burn me, go ahead."

"I didn't—"

She pushed Hitchson against the wall, "*Don't lie to me!*"

He pushed her arms away and, in one swift movement, he put his hands around her neck and shoved her against the bookcase, "I didn't kill anyone. I don't know what happened to Kal."

"The hell you don't," she screamed raspily, his thumbs pressing hard on her neck, making it hard to talk."

"I kidnapped Casey and Anna, you know that, but I didn't kill," he whispered loudly, "I wouldn't kill my victim, that makes them worth less."

Chloe kicked him in the shin and pushed him away from her, coughing, "Then who-" she coughed again, "-did?"

"I don't know," he held his shin.

"You should still be locked up," she spat recklessly.

"Well, lucky for me, the dumb ass who killed Kalvin set me free. Now I'm one step closer to the prize."

"What prize?" She demanded.

He smiled slyly, "Everyone's got a motive, isn't that right?"

She grabbed the stapler, "I'm not even kidding right now, unless you want staples in your face, I suggest you tell me what exactly you're talking about."

He shook his head, laughing to himself, "A stapler, Chloe?"

She opened it and swung at him, almost getting him in the arm.

"Okay, okay, Jesus!" He caved in, backing away nervously, "There's this game. I don't know who started it, but you need at least two people. Because you go against each other, it's a competition. I'm not allowed to know who I'm going against."

"What's the game?"

"To see how many people you can kidnap in a month, but they have to be alive." He answered quickly, eyeing the stapler.

"It's been almost two and a half weeks since Casey. So you've got two people, according to your story?"

He nodded, "Yes."

"What's the prize?"

"Money."

"How much money?"

"A thousand for each person you kidnap. But only to whoever gets more."

Wow. "And if you lose?"

"You get nothing. And if nobody is suspicious of you, you have to kill the ones you kidnapped in order to avoid getting caught. Losing was never an option for me."

"Who's your partner working with you?"

He asked tensely, "How do you know—"

She raised the stapler, threatening him.

"Okay, it was my lawyer."

"That's why you got out so quickly." She shut the stapler and set it down on the desk, "We never had this conversation."

"Agreed."

"Agreed," she nodded, making it official, "Stop kidnapping people."

He stopped her, "Wait. I'll make you a deal. I let Casey and Anna go, and I help you find Kalvin's killer, and you be my kidnapped victim so I win after we get rid of him."

"You think the guy who…is the one you're going against?" She still couldn't bear to say out loud that Kal was killed, it hurt too much.

"Did you see his truck? Dark colored, a tarp over the back?"

"Yeah…." She answered carefully.

"I've been seeing him around. He's been watching me. He wanted you to see him so he could kidnap you. He's stealing my victims."

For a few seconds, Chloe considered his deal, "You and me, working together?" She shook her head, adding, "I don't think I can trust you."

"Look, I can live with getting a thousand dollars out of all this mess. I have a guaranteed shot of winning if you help me, why would I betray you?"

"In a very twisted kinda way, that makes sense."

He nodded, "So, in the end, you've avenged Kalvin's death, I get a thousand dollars, and everyone's free to go."

The bell rang, interrupting their discussion.

"Think about it," Hitchson said.

Expressionless and confused, she walked out of his office, turning back at the doorway, "If you're lying to me…." She trailed off, then began a new sentence, "I guess we've got a deal."

"What's *your* reason for doing this, Miss Johnson?" He asked out of pure curiosity, "I mean, you just shoved me against the wall, got choked, kicked me, and threated to staple my face for information."

"I'm empty." She answered, "I've got nothing to lose." She went to get her books, but when the thought of going to chemistry to an empty chair that belonged to Kal crossed through her mind, she didn't even bother going. She started crying at the thought, so she could only imagine what would happen if she went into the classroom and sat down.

Instead, she just went into the locker room and sat on the floor, leaning against the wall. Nobody had gym first hour, so she wouldn't be bothered. It was impossible for her to accept that Kal was gone. Literally just gone, not even getting a chance to say goodbye. He was never going to walk into the school with his backpack over his shoulder; she was never going to see him. Ever again.

Kal opened his eyes, his head throbbing. All he really remembered was getting hit, and his house was covered in gasoline, then lit on fire in two seconds flat. He remembered seeing Chloe, he tried to yell for her, but he wasn't loud enough. He couldn't get her attention. She looked so terrified. She must be so worried.

He noticed dried up blood that crusted on his forehead, his arms in chains against the wall, legs duct taped together. He was in a small room, maybe the size of a usual bathroom. The walls had blood splatters all over them, the door had scratch marks, there were no windows, the only light in the room came from the dim oil lamp hanging in the farthest corner.

The door opened and a bulky, grim man came in, a box in his arms. He closed the door and turned up the lamp, the flame growing larger, glowing brighter. He reached into the box and took out a lighter.

"Who are you?" Kal begged helplessly, staring at the lighter.

The man took out a metal pole, flicking the flame to the lighter and heating the end of the pole, gloves on his hands.

"Oh, God, please." Kal begged.

After the end of the metal pole was glowing red hot, the man began walking toward Kal, slowly to build the suspense and fear.

"What are you doing?" Kal screeched, "No, please." He flailed his body, chains rattling, "Please stop. Help me!" He yelled, "Help!"

The man enjoyed the sizzling sound of Kal's flesh burning as he carved into it, loving the shrieking yells.

"How many has he kidnapped?" Chloe asked Hitchson as she drove; she had demanded to drive so he couldn't suddenly decide to kill her while they were all alone.

"I'm not sure. A lot. I can't compete."

She felt it strange, talking to a kidnapper about kidnapping. Weeks ago she never would have guessed this would be happening.

He continued, "He's won every game he's played. But after he wins the money, he kills his victims and lays them along ditches. We know it's him because he…carves a brand into them."

"Carves a brand?"

He nodded, "It's the only way the cuts don't bleed, the fire helps…." He stopped.

Chloe stopped the car outside the police station, shaking the thought of a carved burned brand in a dead body out of her mind, "So what's the plan, here? You distract and I peek, or what?"

"You distract. I peek." He corrected, getting out of the car.

"Yeah, of course that's how it goes." She followed him out.

"Can you do that?"

"I think I can pull it off. For Kal." She walked in before him, not wanting the discussion to go on any longer. He waited outside as she went in, talking to the two young police men, "Excuse me. I was wondering...." She paused, because she was completely making everything up as she went, "Do you like...save people's lives?"

The men, who both looked barely over 21, looked at each other, "Yeah," one answered, stepping anxiously toward her, "yeah, we save lives and stuff."

"Have you ever...killed anyone?" She bit her lip and stepped towards them, "'Cause I think that's totally hot." Hitchson knew this was the time to go, so he made his move, running in silently and going into the file room as Chloe went on, "I mean, have you ever had to shoot anyone?"

The cops stood by her, "Well," one said, but the other interrupted.

"I've gotten shot...at before." He added the last part quickly, as if she wouldn't understand it.

Chloe nodded, "Hmm, a guy who dodges bullets? You can be my own personal Superman or something."

The other competed for her attention, "I was in a drug search before."

"Really," she nodded, looking at him.

"I took the dogs back to the car." He answered proudly.

There was a small awkward pause before the wannabe Superman said, "Well, we should get back to…the law and…such."

Chloe added desperately, with a mysterious tone, "Where do you keep your handcuffs?"

One of them got very wide-eyed and smiled, the other just started stupidly at her chest, holding out handcuffs for her to take, grinning. She worried she would have to get him a towel to clean up drool pretty soon.

A crash in the file room broke off their hypnotized faces, but Chloe acted fast as the officers' heads snapped to look. She snatched the handcuffs and put one side on the smarter one's wrist, yanking them closer, taking them by surprise. Then, she pulled him to the floor and wrapped the small chain around the desk let, kicking the dumber officer down and handcuffing him. To finish things off, she unplugged the phone and scooted it out of their reach, the whole time convincing herself she had to assault and trick police officers for Kal.

Hitchson came out carefully, a big file folder in his arms.

"What did you do?" She demanded as they rushed out of the station and back to the car.

"What did *you* do?" He shot back, "You just beat down two police officers."

"They wouldn't stop ogling me, it was pissing me off."

He explained his situation, "I pulled a drawer out too far so it fell."

"That sounds stupid. Now drive fast," she pleaded, looking back to see if anyone was looking as she put on her seatbelt, "I'm now running from the law."

Kal yelled louder as the last part of the brand was sliced and burned into the left side of his chest. He could still feel his skin burn and sizzle as the man walked away, dragging the box out and shutting the door, obviously satisfied with his work. Kal looked at his half-ripped open shirt, looking at the brand on his chest. It said nothing but *GAMER* in all capital letters, all were only about an inch tall and half an inch to an inch wide. His skin was still glowing as he looked away, closing his eyes in pain.

"I'm in a teacher's house," Chloe said, sitting stiffly and looking around, "this is too weird. I mean, even though you aren't really a teacher-teacher, you're a kidnapper-teacher, but it's still weird."

"Enough chit-chat. Let's have a look at the file." He sat down next to Chloe on the couch, setting the file on the coffee table.

"Whose file is this?"

"I took a look at all the John Doe killers, this one has a picture of the brand he puts on his victims, that's the only way I knew it was him." He opened the file and showed her the picture of the chest of a man, the word *GAMER* burned and carved into him.

Her teeth snapped together and she looked away from the picture.

"That's Nothin' compared to how he kills them."

She was afraid to ask, but she did anyway, of course, "Does he…burn them?"

"No," he sounded sympathetic toward her because of Kal's death, "He…. First he cuts off their hands and feet, then he stabs them, so they slowly bleed to death. Then he cuts off their heads and sews them back on…to a different body."

She couldn't open her mouth, she was afraid of what would come out between words and vomit. Hitchson respected this, so he went on reading the file to himself silently, taking in any information on his opponent that he could.

Finally, Chloe asked, "So he killed Kal just so you wouldn't get another victim?"

"That's my guess."

"In a way…I'm glad he killed him. I'm glad he didn't make him go through this torture." She nodded toward the file, a look of disgust on her face.

Hitchson put his hand on her shoulder and spoke softly, "He didn't deserve any of this. I'm truly sorry."

She looked at him, shaking her head, "How did a man like you get mixed up in this? Kidnapping deals and stealing files, I mean."

"What do you mean a *guy like me*?" He laughed lightly, spreading out the contents of the folder onto his coffee table, looking them over.

"You seem so…nice." She couldn't think of any other word to use.

"Yeah, well, so did you. But look what happened after the man you loved was murdered." Her heart stung at his words, and her eyes and throat burned at the word "murder". He looked at her face after she didn't answer, "Exactly my point. You look like you're ready to kill." Turning his body to face hers, he continued, "If you looked at the perfect student, like yourself, for example, you wouldn't ever be able to predict that you'd be slamming your superintendant up against the wall and threatening him with a stapler. There's always something to light someone's fuse."

She saw the glimmer of sadness in his eyes as he looked away, "What happened that lit yours?"

He looked at her like she had just asked the dumbest question in the world, then he got up and walked out of the room, into the kitchen.

"So you can give me the cold hard truth, but I can't know anything you've—"

"Do I act like your councilor?" He yelled suddenly, "If we were really getting to know each other, why don't we start with your father, huh?"

In indignation, Chloe responded by locking her mouth shut as he came back into the living room.

"No matter how much you think you know someone, you can't trust them. You'll figure that out one day." He waited for a response, the silence ringing before he added, "Who knows, you could be just as bad as your father; after all, violence runs in families, it's in your genes, Chloe."

With this, she stood up, putting the papers back into the file.

"What are you doing? Put that stuff down." He coerced.

She tucked it into her hoodie pocket as good as she could, hugging it to protect it from the thick rain, then she looked up and said the only words that were in her mind, "Fuck you."

Kal licked his cracked lips, turning his head to look up at his watch, which told him it was almost 6:00 p.m. How many days had he been kidnapped? Three? Four? He wasn't sure. But it was almost time for the man to come in again, Kal closed his eyes, thinking of the procedure. He would come in and take him out of his restraints to let him go to the bathroom and eat a little, having a couple sips of water before he was chained back up and tortured in a different way. It was different every night, the torture.

The door was shoved open, the man coming in with his Taser gun in hand, taking off Kal's chains and duct tape. If he made one bad move, he would immediately be shot and re-chained without food, water, or a bathroom break, and there would be extra torture. He had never tried anything, but he had been warned.

After he went to the bathroom and ate and drank a little for five minutes, he reluctantly obeyed to being chained back up. The man dug into the box with his gloves on, searching for his object of choice to torture Kal with tonight.

"Please," Kal pleaded, "What'd I do to you!?"

He stood up, a knife in his hand.

"Oh God, no." He squirmed, "Please!" he yelled.

The man started to walk toward him, speaking in his deep, chilling voice, "Pick a place. Arm or leg, which would you rather have stabbed? And why." He rubbed the edge of his blade with his thumb, looking at Kal curiously.

"What?" Kal couldn't believe was he was hearing.

"Answer it." He demanded, watching the flustered Kal squirm. After he didn't answer, he punched him hard, busting open his scabbed lip, "Answer it!"

Kal answered in pain, "I don't know! My...my arm."

The man nodded, then stabbed the knife into Kal's calf, looking at his face as he screamed in agony.

CHAPTER 5

"Kal, what is this?" She tried to touch him, but he was vanishing, his skin felt like water, slipping right through her fingers.

"Chloe," Kal's voice was faint as he faded, gone now, "Chloe, come on. Miss Johnson, wake up!"

Chloe opened her eyes, sitting up quickly, confused by her dream. When she looked over, she saw that Hitchson had busted down her door, "What. The hell?" She asked, still recovering.

"Hurry!" he grabbed the file, "The police are coming, I heard on the scanner at my house—"

She quickly slipped on her sneakers, putting her jacket on at the same time; then, to Hitchson's annoyance, she ran into the kitchen.

"What are you *doing*?" He asked, looking nervously out of the window.

"Shh, you'll wake up my mom, if she's not already awake and calling the cops 'cause *someone* broke down our front door," she warned, climbing onto the counter.

"What on earth are you doing?" He demanded again.

She looked on top of the cabinets, taking down a small box, police sirens in the distance. She quickly jumped down and opened the box, telling Hitchson, "My mom bought this after…." Trailing off, she took out a black as night pistol and slipped the extra bullets into her jeans pocket, glad she had fallen asleep without changing the night before. She zipped up her jacket, putting her hoodie on over it, slipping the gun into her hoodie pocket as she looked at Hitchson, "Let's go."

He led the way, and she grabbed her backpack as they went out the door. They slid into Hitchson's car and calmly and casually drove away, not wanting to draw any extra attention to themselves; after all, the cops were close, the sirens were louder. Triggered by the sounds of the sirens, Chloe saw a small glimpse of her father swinging the gun down on her face. She quickly tried to shake it off.

"You came for me." It wasn't a question, and it didn't even sound like she wanted a response, it was just a statement. After they got far enough away from the scene, the car ride was less tense, and Chloe calmly added, "Why?"

"You're a good kid," he replied plainly.

Loosening her tight grip on the pistol that was in her hoodie, "A good kid with a fuse growing shorter by the second, right?"

He looked at her, "Sometimes revenge isn't such a bad thing. He's a bad man, one who has killed hundreds, Chloe." There was an awkward pause, the hum of the engine being the only constant sound, the occasional ticking of the turn signal being the only other noise until Hitchson finally spoke again, "Your father was the one who lit my fuse."

She looked at him.

He went on, "It was...before he attacked you and your mom. Only a day or two before. My brother was…into drugs and things. Your dad was a lot bigger than him and…"

She could tell it was hard for him; and she wasn't sure she wanted to hear the rest, so she looked away, looking out of the window.

"Jason, my brother, couldn't pay your dad his money on time…."

Chloe shook her head, "I knew my Dad was messed up, but I didn't think…." She stopped, looking at the passing trees and houses.

Her cell phone rang, ringtone singing "I Don't Want to Miss a Thing" by Aerosmith. She quickly answered it, making a mental note inside her head to change the ringtone to avoid future tears, "Hello?"

"Chloe Anne Johnson!"

"Hi, Mom," she said nervously.

"Where are you? Why are the cops showing up at my house? They told me you *stole* confidential files? Where are you? What's going on, Chloe? Why won't you answer me!?"

"Breathe, Mom." Chloe said calmly, "I'll explain later. Don't call again. I love you." She hung up and turned the phone off.

Without warning, police sirens roared and two police cars sped up, chasing them from behind.

"Great." Chloe looked out of the back window.

"Hold on," Hitchson put his arm in front of Chloe to keep her secure as he accelerated quickly, making a sudden right turn.

Kal looked up, surprised to see the man coming into his room. He looked at his watch to see that it was 7:08 a.m. Why was he coming in? He didn't do anything wrong! Why was he coming in off-schedule?

The man obviously saw Kal's confused face, so he felt obliged to explain, "I'm...hunting tonight," he chuckled, "we're doing the routine early. Lucky you."

Kal hung his head, unable to fight. Unable to cry.

"There's a dead end up ahead." Hitchson said, "There's a narrow path, cars can't fit through. We're running for it."

Chloe took off her backpack and shoved the file into it, putting it back on and tightening the straps, putting up her hair with the ponytail holder she had around her wrist.

"I'm gonna block the path with the car, we're getting out my door, got it?"

She nodded, grabbing into the seat as Hitchson turned the wheel, slamming the breaks, causing the car to go into a sideways slide, two trees stopping it, jolting them both. He opened the door, rushing out and holding his hand in for Chloe to take, helping her out.

He held his breath, terrified of what was to come. His only chance was to run for it now, if he didn't run now, while he was free of his chains, he would have to go through more of the hell he was already being put through. It was his only hope. He felt the cut on his calf rip as he ran, warm, fresh blood oozing down his dirty, bloodstained leg.

"Kal!" the voice echoed.

Kal stopped running, for he had been caught. Torture was going to be worse tonight.

Chloe and Hitchson crawled under the barbed wire fence, the police climbing over Hitchson's car. Chloe stood up, hearing Hitchson yell: he was stuck, the sharp barbed wire clinging to his ankle as the cops advanced quickly, guns drawn.

"Stop right there!" They yelled.

Chloe looked at the trail, then at Hitchson, then at the cops. She looked at the trail again, tasting the sweetness of revenge on her tongue as she started to run down it before she decided it wasn't right, and she ran even faster toward Hitchson to help him. She yanked the fence out of his leg and dragged up, helping him stand, giving all the help she could.

"Stop!" the cops ordered.

They refused, running as fast as Hitchson could, Chloe close in front of him, staying close enough to help him if he needed it.

"One more warning, stop or we'll shoot!"

Again, they refused, still running, causing the cops to start shooting.

Kal was chained up, food on a small table out of his reach, adding to his torture. He was already bleeding from the kicks and punches the man had given him earlier. He spat out the blood that gathered in his mouth, the rest just oozing out of his mouth and down his chin, neck, and chest as he yelled angrily toward the ceiling, cursing at his pain.

Hitchson fell to his knees, blood exploding from his throat as a bullet sliced through him. Chloe stopped for a second, but a bullet hit the ground close to her foot, so she ran again, her hand on the gun that was inside her hoodie pocket, breathing quickly. Her mind was in a haze as she ran, she tried forcing the image of Hitchson's death out of her mind, but the image seemed to be stuck to her eyelids.

Finally, she came up to a small house. The yard was bare, and the windows were covered; but the creepy feeling didn't stop her from running in, the door creaking.

"Hello?" She asked quietly, voice shaking. "Hello?"

"Help!" A voice shrieked, "Help me!"

Hitchson's kidnapped victims. Chloe realized now that Hitchson wanted her to find them, to set them free; after all, she agreed to be his only victim so he could win and have the money.

"Where are you?"

There was banging on the wall to her right, so she moved quickly, finding a door. Unlocking it, she opened it, two girls quickly coming out.

"Chloe!" Anna had never been so happy to see her before.

And Chloe had never been so happy to see Anna, "Thank God."

Casey and Anna hugged her, asking, "How did you find us?"

"It's a really long story, but look, you guys have to get out of here."

"Yeah, good idea, come on," Anna grabbed Chloe's arm.

"No," Chloe said quickly, "Just you two."

"Why?"

"The cops are after me, another long story. Just go, okay?"

"Chloe—"

"Anna, trust me, just go. Follow the trail, the cops should be coming this way. But be careful," she warned them, "they could shoot, so make sure you stay down and announce yourselves."

"What are you gonna do?" Anna asked, concerned.

"I have to find someone."

The man watched as Anna and Casey left the house, leaving Chloe all alone. All alone. For his taking.

Kal yelled again, the chains cutting into his wrists. He kept yelling until his throat burned, causing even more pain as he thought about how bland his life was. He had a popular girlfriend in a small town school, his best friend was a girl, he had a rather strange Dad: his life was so normal. Like a movie. And now he was going to die and lose everything.

He remembered the day he met Anna. She was a new student their sophomore year; only a year ago. Chloe was the one who was assigned to show her around....

"Kal," Chloe stopped him in the hallway, "here's that Algebra two homework from the other day," she held the paper out for him.

"No, you don't have to, Chlo."

"You helped me with that retarded English paper, and I kept you up all night on the phone last night, I figured you didn't have your math done. So here." She shook the paper until he finally took it.

"Thanks, but now we're even." He smiled, looking into her eyes.

She smiled back and rolled her eyes, blushing at his amazing smile, "Okay, okay," she bit her lip.

"Miss Johnson," the principal walked up, "this is Anna Wilson, do you mind showing her around today? She's new, she came in from Chicago last week."

"Yeah, sure, no problem," Chloe accepted.

Kal looked at Anna as if she were a shooting star, bright and flashy, like something he had never before seen. She looked back at him and smiled shyly.

Chloe looked at both of them, smile disappearing as she realized he was slipping away. Not able to handle watching them another moment longer, she mumbled something and walked away.

But Kal didn't even notice, "I'm Kal."

"Short for Kalvin?" Anna asked.

"Yeah, but everyone calls me Kal."

"Well I'm not like everyone else. I'll call you Kalvin."

He nodded, studying her face, "Well then Kalvin it is."

Kal coughed, more blood coming out of his mouth, unpleasantly pulling him out of his daydream. He had to get out of here one way or another. He had to try again, even if it kills him.

Chloe was just about to walk out of Hitchson's worn down kidnapping fortress, but someone lurked out of the shadows, so she faced the shadows, backing up a little, putting her finger to the trigger of the gun inside her hoodie pocket, "Who are you?"

"I have Kal, that's all that matters."

"No you don't," she argued, "Kal's dead."

He laughed, "A body is easy to replace, especially when you're me. I just stuck in a different man and took Kal. It was as easy as it'll be to kill you."

"What do you want?" She didn't believe him.

"Where's Hitchson? His only two victims just escaped, and he's not one to give up easily. I didn't get that vibe from him."

"Hitchson's dead."

"That's too bad, he was a moderate competition."

"What do you want?" She asked again.

"To win my game."

"Well. Hitchson's dead now, you won." Her voice shook with fear of how he was looking at her, she knew he wasn't going to let her just walk out of there.

"This is gonna hurt." He warned, rushing to her before she even had a chance to pull the gun from her pocket, shoving a cloth to her face, the scent hard to handle before she fell unconscious.

Kal looked up weakly as the door screeched open, the Gamer coming in, dragging someone by the feet, "What's going on?" He croaked.

The Gamer dragged the person in, turning up the flam on the oil lamp, illuminating the small room with a yellow tinted light.

Kal's heart stopped, "Chloe!"

"Shut up," the Gamer warned, dropping Chloe's feet.

She had blood running down the left side of her face from some sort of a struggle, making Kal's anger grow, rising in his chest. The Gamer bolted more chains to the wall next to Kal, picking Chloe up and chaining her up.

"Please don't," Kal begged for Chloe.

The Gamer duct taped her feet and let her limp body go, "I'll be back with my tools," he told Kal, walking out and shutting the door.

"Chloe," Kal said as soon as the door shut, "Chloe, please, wake up. Chloe, wake up!"

Chloe tried to open her eyes. She could feel chains digging into her wrists, and it hurt, but she was too weak.

"Chloe....Chloe...."

Someone was calling her name, it echoed softly in her head.

"Chloe!"

She opened her eyes slowly and saw a dirty, bloody floor. Her feet were duct taped, and her wrists were chained above her head, which was killing her.

"Chloe." Kal said.

She slowly looked over at him.

"Kal...?"

"Chloe, you've gotta focus, okay? Are you okay?"

Her eyes could only focus on all of the blood that covered him, at all of the pain he was in, "Oh my God, no..." she wept, hanging her head weakly.

"Chloe, this is important, okay? I need you to try something. It's gonna hurt, but you have to trust me."

She shook her head, mind spinning as she looked down at the bloody floor.

"Do you trust me?" he spoke softly.

She closed her eyes and nodded, sniffling quietly.

"Okay, swing your legs up to my hands." He instructed.

"Do what?"

"You have to try, and you have to hurry. He's coming back."

"There's a gun in my hoodie, can you get it?"

"Swing your legs," he said, "and I'll try."

After a few tries, she got her legs to his shoulders, so he took the duct tape off of her ankles with his teeth, spitting it onto the floor. The gun was sticking half-way out of her hoodie pocket, so she was instructed not to move as he pushed his arm as far and hard as he could, his fingertips inching toward the gun....

"Got it," he said, pulling his arm back to a more comfortable position.

Chloe slowly slid her legs off of him, making a muffled "Agh," noise as the chains dug into her wrists, "we need to get these chains off."

"How?"

She eyed the gun in his hand, "shoot them."

"Ha," he shook his head, looking around for a way to get out.

"I'm serious, Kal, shoot the chains off, I trust you."

"Chloe, this is crazy. It's not like Titanic, okay? It doesn't work like that." He shook his head.

"I know, it's different. It's a gun, not an axe."

"This isn't funny, I'm not gonna shoot the chains off of you, what if I miss and shoot your arm off?"

"Then at least I'm out of my chains." She joked, but added quickly at his horrified face, "Kal, just shoot the chains that are way above my arms, okay? You won't hurt me, and we'll get each other out of here."

Seemingly giving up, he aimed the gun as good as possible with his one hand, then shook his head, "Chloe—"

"Kal, I can live without a hand if you screw up! Just shoot or we'll never get out of here and we'll die anyway." She tried desperately to convince him.

Bang!

The chains of one hand fell to the floor, and she hung crooked for a moment by her other hand.

"Are you okay?" he asked quickly, afraid he had shot her.

"Yeah, Kal, I'm fine." She steadied herself and swung slightly, hooking her foot around his leg so she could pull herself over, wrapping her leg around his as she pulled on the chains of his wrists with her free hand.

The Gamer heard the gunshot, gritting his teeth at his mistake of not checking the innocent looking blonde for weapons. He grabbed two guns and a knife, starting back to the room, his bullet proof vest secure and hidden.

One death wouldn't make too big of a difference.

Kal was free of his chains, but his duct taped-together legs caused him to fall as he hit the floor. He tore it off as quickly as possible, and then stood up, putting the gun in his belt as he reached up to help Chloe get her one chained hand free. He held onto her as he helped her stand, bending down and ripping the rest of the duct tape off of her ankles.

The door screeched quickly open, and Chloe and Kal just stood there in shock. The Gamer wasn't the only one standing in the doorway.

There was another.

They stood there calmly, like father and son.

"No…." Chloe mumbled, confusion blinding her.

Aaron Hale walked into the room, "Hi Chloe. Glad you're finally re-united with your lover."

"Aaron?" She asked, as if she were waiting for him to rip off his face, revealing his true identity; because, there was no way Aaron Hale would do this, "Why?"

He laughed, shaking his head, "I gave you plenty of chances, Chlo, but you still ignored me. Even after your precious Kal was reported dead, you were only interested in yourself. It was all about what *you* wanted. All you cared about was him, and you never even gave me a chance."

"Hold on," she tried to understand.

"I would have treated you right, you know that? Not like him, he ignored you. He didn't even have a clue. Kinda like you. I loved you, dammit, and you never saw it."

"Aaron, I…."

"No, it's too late for that."

"But how…?"

Aaron explained, "He told me about the game. As I sat all alone on our awesome little *double date*."

"Look, Aaron—" Kal tried.

"You shut up," Aaron growled.

"We don't need to explain anything," The Gamer said, "and we don't need chains to detain you," he told Kal and Chloe as they walked out and shut the door, the sound of clicking locks following, then something heavy slammed against it.

But Chloe didn't care. She threw her arms around Kal and held him close, her head on his shoulder as he gently and weakly held her with one arm. For once, these were happy tears that streamed from her eyes, running down her face as she held him tighter, never wanting to let go.

She spoke into his shoulder, "You were dead," she wept, "we had your funeral and e-every thing." She stuttered with emotion, sniffling.

Why the hell are you here? How?" he rested his chin on to top of her head, "And where did you get a gun?"

"I was looking for your killer." She answered honestly.

He backed away from her, looking into her eyes, "Why would you do that?"

Because I'm in love with you, dummy. No, that's too over the top. Okay, I love you. That'll work. Say it. Say I love you. "You're my best friend." *What? That was not the plan.* She fought with herself.

He shook his head, eyes admiring her, "You're insane, you know that?"

"I'm gettin' there," she agreed with a laugh, which disappeared quickly as she saw the brand that was carved into his chest. She mumbled the name, wishing it wasn't true.

"How does Hitchson tie into all this?" Kal wondered aloud, sitting down on the dirty floor, pulling up his pant leg carefully and slowly to look at the stab wound.

"He-eew." She stopped when she saw the wound, sitting down next to him, trying to ignore the disgusting floor, "Are—"

"I'm okay," he answered before she could finish asking.

A faint yell erupted from the other side of the wall they were leaning against, causing Chloe to jump, Kal just gritted his teeth.

"What's going on?" Chloe asked, looking at Kal's face.

He hesitated, "Let's just hope he doesn't come in here next."

Chloe nodded, looking fearfully at the door.

CHAPTER 6

There was a loud, sudden bang on the door, so Kal and Chloe both stood up. She grabbed onto his wrist with one hand, watching the door open slightly.

"Aaron's voice was the only thing that came in, "Kal, go to the furthest corner. Chloe, come to the door with the gun in you jeans pocket, hands up."

"Go to hell," Kal refused.

Aaron laughed again, "You have no clue what you're dealing with, Kalvin. Or how much you've hurt her. Anything any of us do to her won't be nearly as bad, I promise you."

He looked at Chloe, confused.

"Just do as I say or you both die, how 'bout that?" He sounded bored.

She looked at Kal and slowly took the gun from his hand.

He shook his head, "I don't think this is a good idea, Chlo."

She stuck the pistol into her pocket, inching toward the door.

"In the corner, Kal," Aaron ordered bitterly.

Kal clenched his jaw tightly and backed away; but, if looks could kill, Aaron would have been dead as soon as they saw him standing next to the Gamer.

As Chloe reached the door, it opened quickly; although it all seemed to be going in slow motion: Chloe pulled the gun from her pocket, putting her finger on the trigger. It was like Aaron expected it, because his arm shot out and grabbed the gun, punching Chloe in the stomach to make her let go before she could shoot. All at the same time, the Gamer ran in, slamming Kal against the wall, making him watch as Aaron pushed Chloe to the floor, raising the gun into the air, looking over at Kal and grinning the most evil grin imaginable.

"Remember this?" He asked, swinging the gun hard, hitting her in the face with it over and over, then he spoke to Chloe, still swinging, "Your lover comforted you then, why not now?" He swung harder, faster.

The Gamer kneed Kal in the stomach, walking out with Aaron as they laughed like buddies. Buddies who had just simply won a harmless football game; because to them, this was a game. They were having fun.

Kal staggered as if drunk, the sharp pain enabling him. He could barely stand, let alone walk as he stumbled as fast as possible over to Chloe. "Chl-" he fell to the floor, clutching his stomach, coughing.

Chloe couldn't get the images out of her head, even if she closed her eyes, all she saw was the gun, her father, the gun again, Aaron, the gun once more, her father....

Kal crawled using his elbows to drag himself, getting onto his hands and knees once he reached her, "Chloe," he grabbed her shoulder and rolled her over onto her back.

She was trying not to cry, her forehead and jaw bone scratched deeply. She was more terrified than anything else, eyes wide, the flashes of faces and guns like a slideshow on fast-forward in her mind.

"Hey," Kal was scared, he had never seen her like this before, he was afraid she was going into shock, "Chloe, hey," he pulled her onto his lap.

She slowly regained the ability to see reality, seeing Kal's face close to hers, "Kal," she muttered dreamily.

"Hey," he forced a grin, "You're okay," he stroked her hair, pushing it out of her bloody face.

"Haven't we been here before?" She barely moved her mouth to talk, the cuts squirting out more blood.

"Shh," he instructed, "don't talk, okay?"

She closed her eyes.

"And don't fall asleep," he rushed.

She opened her eyes, eyelids heavy.

"You have to stay conscious. You'll be fine."

"Kal," she tried, "I can't…."

"You can," he nodded, "stay awake."

She fought hard to keep her eyes open.

"You can, dammit." He shook her slightly as her eyes fluttered closed.

When Chloe opened her eyes, she was lying on the floor, but on some type of cloth. Her head was resting on her backpack and her hoodie was off of her, on top of her, serving as a blanket. She looked up, seeing Kal standing over by the chains on the other side of the room. He was shirtless, bruised, and red; not exactly how she imagined he would be with his shirt off. She looked down, realizing the cloth she was lying on was his shirt.

He collected the longest chains, planning to use them as weapons if he had to, turning around and seeing Chloe as she sat up, "Tell me something," he said, "are you sending off some sort of vibes to everyone, telling them to hurt you?"

"Well, if I am, it's working." She said huskily, still barely moving her mouth because she could still feel the pain.

He threw the chains down next to her backpack, sitting down by her as she looked at his bruised body, then up at his bloody face.

He assured her quietly, "I'm okay."

"What did he do to you?" It came out in a whisper, almost silent.

Looking down, he changed the subject, "What all d'you got in that bag?"

Chloe stared at him. Even when he was all bloody, bruised, and dirty, he was still just as amazing as ever. Here he was, he had just gone through the hell factory trials, and here *he* was nursing *her*. He helped her when she needed him, even though nobody was here to help him when he needed it.

For a brief second as she stared at him, she imagined kissing him, just to see how he would react. Kissing is not a hard thing to do. Just move toward him, and put your lips on his; it doesn't even have to be a *good* kiss, just kiss him. She had already lost him once, it won't hurt as bad if she lost him again. At least this time she would have the comfort of knowing he was still alive.

She imagined his fingertips on her face. His lips touching hers. She imaged hearing him say all of the words she had always longed to hear. She imagined him loving her just as she had always loved him; but half as much would do just fine, as long as he loved her back.

If she did kiss him, the worst-case-scenario would be that he never talked to her again, thinking it would be too awkward. The best-case-scenario would be that they confessed their love for each other and would live happily ever after. In a big castle with a dragon as a pet. But fairy-tales don't come true, and she knew that as she looked down.

"You okay, Chlo?" He tore her out of her dreamland, "Are you still seeing the flashes?" He questioned carefully.

"No," she answered quickly, "And how do you know I was—"

"You mumble and…and cry in your sleep," he looked down, "you cried about a lot of things."

"I-about what? What kind of things?"

He shrugged, "Your dad….Aaron, Hitchson, your mom. This Gamer guy. Me."

Crap.

"I talked about you?" She tried to keep the nervousness from her voice, watching his face for any sign that he knew.

He nodded, "You kept saying you didn't wanna lose me, but that you had to tell me."

"Tell you...what?"

"I don't know. That's all you said." He finished with a tease, "You're not gonna end up being a psycho killer that's secretly working with Hitchson through all this, are you?"

"You...never know." She laughed nervously, wondering if she should tell him about the deal with Hitchson.

He pulled the bag over to him, "What'cha got in here?"

"Stuff," she answered, "you can look."

He unzipped it, pulling out the file, "What's this?"

"The stuff the cops had on the Gamer."

He paused, "And how'd *you* get it?"

She hesitated, trying to find an easier, less criminal way to put it, "....That kinda ties in with the long story thing."

Kal opened the file, looking over the papers, "Well all we have is time...." He trailed off, lost in the papers for over ten whole minutes before he spoke again, "This guy's sick."

She nodded, agreeing, "No arguments there."

He set the file down and peeked into the bag again, pulling out a perfectly straight paper, looking at it. It was the invitation to his funeral, with his school picture on the front, his name above it.

Chloe's mouth formed a straight line, and she looked away from the picture, "Everyone was there," she told him, "even Alex. He seemed...pretty torn up, actually."

He put the invitation down, "Just pretend it was all a dream. Even this, when we get out of here. It was all just one big huge painful bad dream."

"A dream I never, ever wanna have again." It almost sounded like a warning.

She couldn't help but find Kal's chest and abs distracting. She tried looking at his face when she looked at him, but sometimes her eyes just...slipped. He never noticed, he was too intrigued by the information in the file, so she let herself look for a little while longer before deciding to refocus her attention to the cuts on her face

She touched the one on her jaw bone, feeling the scab. It was only slightly wet with blood, but it stung when she touched it, so she quickly retracted her hand from her face, glancing at Kal to see if he noticed. When she knew he didn't notice, she touched the cut that was on her forehead, which wasn't quite as deep, and it was fully scabbed, no stinging.

The distraction didn't work for long; as her brain trailed off in thought, it hopped back into the Kal train. Suddenly, something sunk into the world of realization. She was trapped. Trapped with Kal. Alone. Alone with Kal. A shirtless Kal, at that.

"So did Hitchson kidnap Anna and Casey?"

He sure did know how to shoot down her thought bubble.

"Yeah, uh, long story short: he let them go." She decided to just tell him the truth, to try to explain everything, "Err, he had...*me* let them go."

"Wh-...What?"

"Don't freak out, okay? It's a complicated story." She looked at him carefully.

"I...okay. But *Hitchson*?"

"After you were reported dead, I kind of...went a little crazy. Not literally, of course, but I was so numb that nothing really mattered anymore. So, I um...."

"Go on," he urged.

"I went into Hitchson's office and locked the door. We argued and threatened each other, but when I asked him why he killed you, he said it wasn't you. Then he told me about this game."

"This is a game?"

She nodded, "The way I understand it, there's two people playing at a time. The opponents kidnap people, and whoever has the most at the end wins, and they get certain about of money for each victim."

Kal shook his head, stomach sick.

"That guy out there, he's the Gamer. He's the one who like *invented* this whole thing. He wins every single time, so he doesn't ever owe anyone money, but he kills his kidnapped victims afterwards. Apparently it's been going on for a while, according to the file. He's killed...hundreds."

"So this Gamer guy is competing with Hitchson?"

Chloe went on, "Hitchson made me a deal. If I help find the Gamer and help kill him, he would let Anna and Casey go. So, we…worked together to steal the police file. The cops were coming after us, so he was taking me to the place where he kept Anna and Casey. The cops shot and killed him"

Kal looked surprised, keeping quiet as she went on.

"I kept going, and I found them, they're safe now. But the Gamer found me, and he brought me here."

There was a long silence. During this silence, Kal put everything back into the backpack, checking his watch occasionally. Meanwhile, Chloe discovered a huge bruise on her cheekbone, and another one on the bridge of her nose. Wondering if it was broken, she looked up as Kal stood and walked over to the table of food.

"Wonder if he poisoned this…."

She stood up and walked over to the table, looking at the cut-up meat and the bread slices, "And *I* wonder if this is animal or human."

He made a disgusted face, then picked up the three bread slices, "Surely these are okay, right?" He stared at one for a few seconds longer, then took a bite, chewing slowly. When he didn't fall over dead, he handed the other two to Chloe. She took one slice, taking a careful bite.

"Here," he finished his slice, trying to hand her the extra one.

"You, you've been in here for a long time, you should eat more." She insisted.

Kal opened his mouth to argue.

"Eat it." She directed, not taking no for an answer.

He folded it in half and took a bite, most of the slice disappearing.

As he chewed, Chloe asked, "What time is it?"

He looked at his watch, swallowing, "Well, it's been one a.m. for a while now."

"Oh, great." She commented.

"Yeah," he agreed with her sarcasm, followed by another silence as they gradually made their way back to the little bed of clothes Kal had made for her, sitting back down.

Chloe crossed her arms, goose bumps covering her arms from underneath the hoodie she was covering up with, "Aren't you cold?" Her teeth chattered as she looked at him.

He shrugged, "A little."

"Do you want your shirt back?"

"Nah, it's covered in blood anyway," he answered.

She uncovered and put her hoodie back on, putting her hands into her pocket, "How on earth are you not freezing?"

"Guess I'm used to it by now," he changed the subject, "You should sleep."

"*I* should sleep? Are you no longer sleeping?" she asked, "Have you kicked that habit?" she smiled.

He smiled too, unknowingly making her heart stop. He looked into her eyes, making her head spin. He looked at each cut on her face, as if in pain himself, then looked back into her eyes warm-eyed himself, as if he was healing her. He looked from one eye to the other, his smile fading to a grin, which almost caused her to faint.

A loud bang in the room next to them made them both jump, and faint voices were heard, "Freeze! Police!"

Kal and Chloe looked at each other, then they both stood up and ran to the door, banging on it and yelling, "Help! Over here, help! Help us!"

There was a dinging sound, faint but repetitive, followed by the loudest bang they had ever heard as they were thrown by an invisible force, along with the wall and door, orange hot light surrounding them.

The building had exploded.

Kerri Smith

CHAPTER 7

Kal didn't want to open his eyes; for he could feel something heavy on top of him, and a warm liquid spilling down his legs. He moved his arm, feeling sharp edges of the busted up wall. He was stuck, he couldn't move.

Chloe's head throbbed, her scabs were ripped open, her arm felt strange, and sharp pains were spiraling up and down her shoulder. It had to be out of place or broken, it hurt too much to be okay.

She sat up, pushing a chunk of wall off of her leg, looking around. Everything was smoking, and small fires were burning selective things in many different places.

"Kal?" She asked, looking around her, "Kal!?" Her echo followed twice as she stood up and stumbled around, trying to get her footing. *Not again,* she thought, *I can't go through all that again,* "Kal!"

Bodies were poking out of many different places, some of which were dead, others were questionable.

"Kal!" She screamed again, tripping over someone's leg and falling, scraping her arm on a sharp, rough piece of wall.

"Chloe."

The voice was faint, making Chloe wonder if it was just her imagination.

"Chloe, I'm over here."

This time it couldn't be wishful thinking, "Kal?" She stopped, looking around to try to figure out where the noise was coming from.

"Chloe!"

"Where are you?"

"I'm under something!"

"Tell me what you see." She instructed.

"I see wall." He answered.

"Okay, smart-ass, I see wall too. Where are you?" She looked around helplessly.

"I'm trapped under wall pieces, Chloe. All I see is wall. I...I see Aaron, he's right by me."

As Kal said this, someone stood up about ten yards away from Chloe.

She knelt down, grabbing a smaller chunk of wall, demanding, "Who are you?"

The boy looked at her, "I'm-I'm Nathan." He held his bleeding arm, "Please don't kill me."

She looked away dismissively, dropping the piece of brick, back on her search for Kal, "Kal," She yelled again, "I need you to tell me what you see so I can try to find you. You're gonna have to try harder."

"Chloe, I'm *under stuff.*"

She looked down, holding very still, "Am I standing on you?"

"I highly doubt that," he answered, "will you hurry, please? I can't move, and—"

"I'm trying, Kal," she answered as she got down on her hands and knees, "I'm just afraid to move stuff, what if it collapses on you?"

All around her, she heard people groaning and crying in pain, seeing them stand up out of the corner of her eyes, Nathan walking toward them to try to help Chloe.

"I dunno, but—Agh!"

A few feet in front of her, things collapsed, sinking farther down.

"Kal," she was picking up rocks and wall pieces now, not worried about anything collapsing, because they already had. Now her main focus was to get the debris off of him, so she threw piece after piece, eyes looking for any sign of him.

Nathan was there to help as he realized the situation. They dug together, for what seemed to be five whole minutes; the longest five minutes of Chloe's life. Chloe dug faster as she heard a cough, uncovering his face. She could feel her fingers bleed as she shoved the brick off of him, picking up the heavier pieces. She returned to his face, brushing dust off of his mouth and nose.

"Kal," she pulled him slightly so he was completely out from under everything as Nathan still pushed a few bricks away before grabbing Kal's other arm, helping to pull him out of the mess, looking at Chloe as if she were stupid; Kal definitely looked dead.

Chloe was not going to take dead for an answer.

"Kal!" Her voice screeched, caused by her effort to hold in her tears, "Kal, answer me right now," she clenched her jaw, shaking him.

Nathan put his hand on her shoulder, and she let him pull her back into a sitting position. As she put her head in her hands, blood from her fingers stuck to her hair, which burned her cuts; but she didn't care. It didn't matter. Nothing mattered.

Kal coughed, making Nathan jump, backing up a little, but not Chloe. Her head shot up and she looked at him, immobile. Was that real? He coughed again, and this time, Chloe was at his side in half a second flat.

"Baby?—Err, Kal?"

His eyes fluttered open, "You found me."

It wasn't a matter of thinking anymore, this wasn't a logical situation. Everything about this situation was illogical. This was just Chloe, nothing else. She didn't even think ahead, ahead to what the possible outcomes were, all that mattered was the moment. It didn't matter to her anymore about what was going to happen.

She leaned down and kissed Kal, a tear dripping onto his cheek from her eye. At first, he seemed to be in shock, so she began to pull away, realizing the mistake she had just made, but then he surprised her. As the moment sunk in, he responded in a way she always hoped would happen. The smell of the fire, the smoke, the sound of the people in pain, all of it disappeared because of how Kal responded. He kissed her back.

Nathan looked around, scratching his head, trying his best to stay out of the love story that was erupting at his feet. As Kal and Chloe's kiss broke, she kept her eyes closed, afraid to open them. What if, when she opened her eyes, she woke up? She changed her mind, she didn't want all of this to be a dream. She wanted this moment to last forever; but, her wish was soon shot down.

A bullet broke through Nathan's head, blood and brains spattering out onto the pieces of wall and brick beside Kal, making them both jump. As Nathan's body fell to the ground, Chloe looked behind her at where the bullet came from, spotting the Gamer. He was in a tree stand on the other side of where the building used to be, with what Chloe guessed was a sniper rifle of some sort, and he aimed it their way.

She quickly ducked down, covering her head as Kal worked up his strength, rolling onto his stomach. He spotted Aaron's truck, which was parked only half a football field away; they could make it if they ran, if luck was on their side, protecting them from the bullets of the sniper rifle.

"Chloe," he choked huskily.

She looked over at his, then followed his gaze to the truck, "He's got a sniper rifle, Kal. Aah!" She scooted closer to him as a bullet hit a few feet from her head.

"And he's not a very good shot, which is great for us."

She looked back at the Gamer, who was aiming and shooting somewhere else. Obviously, he thought he had hit her, and Kal looked dead enough.

"Fine, let's hurry. We won't have much time." She stood up slowly, staying crouched down as to not draw attention, pulling Kal up with her.

They walked slowly, until they were about half way to the truck and Kal jumped, hearing a bullet whiz past his ear, making him stumble over, taking Chloe down with him.

"Run!" Kal ordered.

She grabbed his arm and used most of her strength to pull him up, putting his arm around her neck, running as he limped desperately beside her.

"Come on," she urged, glancing back behind her at the Gamer, who was reloading, "shit, hurry, Kal."

"I'm trying," he grimaced, sweating, mostly because of pain.

The Gamer had his mind fully focused on Chloe and Kal now, bullets whizzed past them over and over, until finally, one ripped right through Chloe's right arm. She held in a scream, causing a small, strange noise to burn her throat as she clenched her teeth together, still running.

"What happened?" Kal panted.

"Nothing," she lied, voice strained, "just run, okay?"

"Are you shot?"

The grass exploded out of the ground as another bullet hit it only a few feet beside Chloe, another bullet grazing Chloe's leg.

\"Son of a...." she trailed off, falling onto one knee, quickly getting up and supporting Kal.

He locked arms with her, and they both used each other to limp and run the rest of the way to the truck as the Gamer reloaded again. Kal only let go of Chloe when he opened the door to the driver's side of the truck, helping her in before the crawled in behind her, shutting the door as the side mirror was shot off. He started the truck, stepping on the gas as another bullet shattered his window, making glass shower in before they peeled out, speeding away as fast as the truck would carry them.

"That guy," Kal shook his head, spitting a small mouthful of dirty blood out of the broken window, "he's…there's something wrong with him."

Chloe agreed with a sharp hissing sound from the pain in her arm as she slowly and carefully took off her hoodie to tend to her shot arm. Then she took off her jacket, both of which were covered in blood on her right sleeve. After those were off, she took off her shirt, a tank top underneath. Using the shirt, she wiped most of the blood off of her arm.

"Is he following us?" Kal asked, eyes on the road.

She looked back for a few seconds, finally answering, "No," before continuing to tend to her arm.

"Are you okay? You're leg is bleeding, too." He glanced over at her, looking back at the road every few seconds.

"I'll get to that, it just grazed it I think."

"What about your arm?"

"Shot all the way through," she observed, clenching her teeth together in pain, reaching for the glove compartment, "Aaron had to have some sorta pills in here, he was psychotic, after all."

"We should go to the hospital. I know you're wanted by the law and stuff, but if we explain everything to them, they'll believe us. I mean, I'm supposed to be dead. And you're all shot up and stuff."

"*Shot*, Kal. I'm *shot*. I'm not on drugs. You almost ruined our whole story." She laughed.

He laughed too, rubbing at his scratched face, one hand on the wheel.

"What's this?" Chloe pulled a bag out of the glove compartment.

Kal looked at it, then looked out at the road again, "That. Is weed."

She slowly put it back where she had found it, "Lovely."

He laughed at her lightly, resting comfortably in his seat as he drove, trying to ignore all of the different bloody and scabbed wounds on his body.

There was a short silence before she spoke again, "Stop at the police station first."

"But you're bleeding...." He objected.

"Yes, I know, but we have to tell them everything first, then we can go to the hospital. With the file in ashes, we need help, Kal. The police can help if we tell them what the Gamer looks like, and that he's probably gonna be after us."

"Alright, we'll stop there first. But then straight to the hospital."

"Deal."

Another silence followed, and during it, Chloe tied her jacked up around her arm to apply constant pressure and to stop the bleeding, as she peeked through the rips of her jeans at the wound on her leg.

"Chloe, about what happened." He stopped.

"What do you mean?" She asked, urging him on as she left her leg alone, looking over at him trying to ignore the pain.

"I mean…the kiss."

"Oh," she was surprised, because she had forgotten that it had actually happened, "Um…."

"I just wanted to apologize."

"Apologize? No, you don't need to do that, Kal."

"Yeah, I do." He argued, "I mean, you…." He paused and scratched his head awkwardly.

"Where is this going? Kal—"

He interrupted her, "Chloe, no, I have to say this."

"Kal," she refused, "I kissed you. I-I though you died. Twice, to make things worse. But you have nothing to apologize for. You don't have to apologize for kissing me back."

"Will you shut up for two seconds?" He immediately apologized, "I'm sorry, you're just…not stopping. I only apologized because I don't this to be like a big deal," he said reasonably.

"Neither do I." She was very close to suggesting driving back to the Gamer, she preferred bullets to this at the moment, "So why are you making it out to be?"

The last part slipped out, and after she said it, she had to think about whether or not it actually came out, or if she had just thought it.

"I don't mean to," he defended himself.

"You're just so...." She stopped herself, finishing the thought in her head. *Stupid. You're so stupid. I love you, dammit.* "I harassed a teacher to find you. I seduced and beat down two cops. I stole a confidential file, watched Hitchson's head get shot off, crawled under a barbed wire fence, got *kidnapped by the Gamer*, took two really painful bullets to guard you; I risked everything for you. But you still don't get it."

"What don't I get, Chloe?" He asked desperately.

She laughed, mostly in anger, looking out of the window. The silent treatment was the only solution to this problem, she figured. Kal gritted his teeth and turned sharply, causing Chloe to bump into her door and window. She instantly glared at him, eyes narrow, but he pretended not to notice.

Without warning, shots were fired, blowing out one of the back tires, resulting in the truck's uncontrollable swerve, forcing it into an unavoidable roll.

Bang. Thud, thud, bang.

Chloe tried to move.

Thud, thud, bang, thud, thud, bang!

She fought to open her eyes, the annoying noise echoing in her battered head.

Bang, thud, thud, thud.

Her eyes fluttered open, vision blurred.

Bang, bang, thud...bang!

She saw Kal banging on the glass with his fist and elbow. They were in a car, a police car. She sat up, *"What happened?"*

He looked at her, "I don't know. I woke up in here. The stupid Gamer guy just parked the car here and left. I don't even know where he is," he glanced around outside of the car nervously, appearing to by hyperventilating, but that was too much to handle right now, so Chloe prayed that he wasn't.

She looked at the front two windows, which were cracked for air, which was good. They wouldn't die...anytime soon. Her shirt was still tied around her arm, and her leg ached, but she didn't dare to look at it. The good news was: she felt no wet blood anywhere else, so most wounds must have been scabbed up by now. At least she wasn't going to die from blood loss; but she would die from an infection in her wounded arm if she didn't get out of there.

Mrs. Johnson was still in the police station, time rolling around to the 24 hour mark.

"And the boy's mother?" the police man asked.

"She flew in for the funeral, but she's gone now." Chloe's mother told them, crossing her off of the suspect list, "I'm telling you, she just left. She told me...she'd explain later. I tried calling again, but she turned off her phone. She stole a file, why don't you people look at what file she stole! That could give you a lead, right?"

"Do you have any ideas why Chloe would steal files, Mrs. Johnson?"

"No, that's why you should look into it." She snapped.

"Any idea why she'd tie me up?" I disgruntled young policeman yelled from outside the room.

"Excuse him," the policeman talking to her said, rolling his eyes.

"Just please. Find my daughter."

The door swung open, someone talking fast, "There was an explosion, we found bodies. *Lots* of bodies, I think it may have been the Gamer's killing space, and where he kept his vics."

"Any witnesses?"

"They're all dead."

"It's getting dark." This was the first time Kal had spoken in quite a while.

Chloe nodded, agreeing, then bringing up what had been on her mind since the silence began, "Kal…can we just pretend that I didn't kiss you?"

He nodded, "Yeah. That's probably the best idea. With Anna…."

That stab hurt worse than any gunshot ever could. "Yeah," she pretended to agree.

"Can I ask you a question?"

"No, Kal, you cannot." She answered sarcastically, looking at him with her warm, loving eyes.

He grinned, leaning against the door, looking back at her. But before he could reply, the door was ripped open and he fell out backwards. If it wasn't such a serious moment, Chloe most likely would have laughed, because it was a funny sight. But, this was a serious time, because the mystery of *who* ripped the door open was questionable. She definitely didn't laugh; instead, she dove and grabbed onto Kal's leg, until she realized nobody was pulling him or trying to drag him away. They looked at each other, Kal up from the ground and Chloe down from inside the car, both of them confused.

Nobody was there.

They stood up, Chloe getting out of the car, then they looked around wearily.

"I'll find both of you," the Gamer's voice whispered, "and I will kill you."

Police sirens were audible in the distance.

"What?" Chloe looked around, grabbing onto Kal's arm for comfort, "This—"

"Isn't right," Kal finished her sentence, looking around, too, his arm in front of her for protection, fists clenched and ready for a fight.

"Is he—"

"Letting us go? I don't know." He did it again.

"Okay, that's very annoying," she informed him, voice shaking with fear as every noise around her scared her.

"Sorry."

The sirens got closer, and eventually the cops came, guns drawn. Chloe feared for their lives. The Gamer always had extra moves up his sleeves, what if this was a part of his plan, to kill all of them at once? She waited for pain, the pain of another bomb.

There was no bomb.

There were no shots fired.

There was no Gamer.

CHAPTER 8

One Week Later:

Finally.

Chloe never thought she would be *glad* to go back to school. She had gotten out of the hospital a couple of days ago, but the trauma hadn't changed her mother. She was happy Chloe was back, but she was still silent. Still distant.

She went outside, her new backpack on one shoulder, ready to walk to school, surprised to see a small car stopped on the curb, Anna standing outside it, leaning against it as she waited for her.

When they spotted each other, Anna gave a small wave, "Come on, I'll give you a ride."

"Actually, you know, I can walk...." She found this too weird.

"Please, Chloe?" She sounded desperate, like she needed someone to talk to.

She accepted, walking over to the shiny car and getting into the passenger's seat, sitting awkwardly as she waited for Anna to speak, knowing she had to have an ulterior motive for offering her a ride.

After Anna started the car and drove to the stop sign, she began, "Thanks for saving me, it was...." She struggled with the thought of complimenting Chloe, "Well, let's just say I wouldn't have had the guts to do it."

"I wasn't really acting on bravery, Anna."

She nodded, "I know. You weren't doing it for me, it was for Kal."

Chloe quickly argued, "No, I though Kal was—"

"Dead, yeah, I heard. But all you wanted was to find the guy who killed him. Don't get me wrong, I'm glad you did, or else Kalvin would probably be dead for real right now."

Not knowing what to say, Chloe just looked out of the windshield, watching as the school steadily got closer.

"Listen," Anna said as they pulled into the parking lot, "Kalvin told me what happened between you two."

Kal, I'm gonna kill you. "He told—What do you mean?"

"He told me how much you looked after each other. I'm glad he's got a friend like you."

Oh, look, you're both in denial. Joy to the freakin' world. "Thanks, Anna."

Anna got out, Chloe doing the same, and they walked inside together, without any other words being said.

As soon as she walked into the door, everyone froze, looking at Chloe. She tried to hide the scars on her chin and forehead, and her cast on her arm seemed to grow, screaming "Look at me! Look at me!" She looked down, cheeks flushing. She could hear the whispers as she tried to walk faster to get away from them, but they followed her.

"She killed Hitchson,"

"Look at her face, do you see those cuts?"

"She got shot, that's what the cast is from."

"Do you think she has a gun?"

"No, stupid. You can't bring guns in here."

"But she like...breaks the law."

"She killed Hitchson, and she saved Kal, isn't that crazy?"

"Dude, she's crazy."

"Definitely."

She closed her eyes, trying desperately to block them out.

"Did you hear about Aaron?"

"Yeah, he's the one that hit her."

"Did she kill him, too?"

"He did that to her face?"

"Good thing it's small."

"I bet she killed him."

"Stop," Kal's voice came from behind Chloe and Anna, "Mind your own business." He clenched his jaw angrily, backpack on one shoulder.

People slowly began to move again, chattering progressing in volume.

"Are you—?" He stopped as Chloe walked away, pushing through the crowds as they all stared.

"She'll be fine," Anna comforted.

He shook his head, "No. She won't. I have to go talk to her."

"Wait, Kal, I need to talk to you for at least five minutes, okay? I was kidnapped, and you almost died. Can we have two minutes before you run off to go find *her*?"

"Hold on," he started to walk away, going around her.

"I was kidnapped, too, Kal." She tried desperately to keep his attention.

Chloe went into the empty gym yet again. She laid down on the bleachers, hoping that maybe nobody would see her there; nobody would stare. Nobody would whisper. Kal cam in silently and sat down next to her.

"Are you okay?"

She looked at him, sitting up.

"Do you wanna go home?" He suggested.

She didn't answer at first, then she answered silently by shaking her head.

"Are you sure? I'll drive you."

She didn't answer; she just looked at the way he was sitting. The small cast on his leg made him look very awkward, and she could tell he still had many, many bruises.

"You wanna go?" He asked again after she didn't answer.

She shook her head again, speaking this time, "My mom'll just...." *That was a stupid thing to say.* Chloe thought, angry at herself. It was stupid to say, especially now; now that Kal had no parents, and here she was refusing to go back to hers. "Sorry," she mumbled.

"We could go to my aunt and uncle's house."

"Is that where you're staying now?" She asked lightly.

"Yeah, they're really cool," he rubbed her shoulder sympathetically, "wanna go?" he pressed again.

"I'm okay," she shook her head, "really."

"Then at least let me go beat everyone up," he joked, smiling.

"I don't think you'll be beating anyone up in your condition," she frowned, then gently touched the part of his chest that was carved and burned.

"It doesn't hurt anymore," he assured her, "and we can leave at any time. It's up to you, okay?"

"Thanks," she nodded twice, "but it's gonna be like this for a while. Might as well ride it out," she convinced herself more than him.

He frowned.

"What?" She asked, worried she said something.

"I thought you didn't like roller coasters, missy."

She rolled her eyes and mock punched his arm, and he smiled and leaned in, kissing her forehead.

"If you need anything, just find me." He stood up.

She reached up, holding out her hands for him to help her up, "Thanks, buddy."

"C'mon," he encouraged, putting up his fists as if to fight, "let me hit at least *one* of them?" He slow-motion punched the air, only centimeters from her head.

She laughed, pushing his wrist down, then she ruffled his hair with her hands, "Calm down, Balboa."

"Okay," he stood completely still, like a statue.

"I didn't say *shut* down," she smiled.

"Oh, right, sorry."

"What's up?" Anna came in.

"Kal's having identity crises." Chloe informed her with a laugh.

"I am *not!*" He whined like a little boy.

She laughed with him, but she was starting to worry, giving him a *what's wrong with you?* look, so he stuck his tongue out at her.

"And now he's apparently having a bit of an age crisis," she whispered loudly to Anna.

He laughed, going back to Kal: age 17, "Okay, I'm good now."

"Glad you got that out of your system."

Anna was just silent, awkwardly nodding and laughing, trying to join into the conversation.

The bell rang, so Kal and Chloe both walked past Anna, who stood there shaking her head for a moment before she went off to her first class, face hot as she watched her boyfriend with Chloe.

"Hey, wait up," he said to Chloe, "I'll walk you to class." He acted like her bodyguard, holding onto her shoulder and leading her quickly through the crowd.

In chemistry, Kal gave a frightening death-stare to anyone who even glanced at her, acting as more of a terrifying guard dog now, rather than a body guard. But still, the stares didn't stop the whispers.

"How'd it happen?"

"I think she shot Hitchson."

"Yeah, they say his head was blown off."

"At least she saved Anna 'n Casey."

"Then she found that place where the Gamer was hiding."

"Yeah, and she blew it up."

"She killed all those cops and them kidnapped people."

"Why would she do that?"

"Maybe it was meant to be suicide, too."

"Maybe she just likes the attention."

Kal stood up, chair flinging and clanking onto the floor, silencing everyone, "If I have to say it *one more time,* I swear—"

"Kal, sit." Chloe tried quietly.

"Kalvin," the teacher warned.

"Why is he even on her side? Didn't she try blowing him up, too?"

"Maybe they're working together or something."

"Shut the hell up!" He yelled, looking at the group where the whispers came from, stepping toward them threateningly, "Just shut up."

"Kalvin," the teacher scolded, "we will not have that kind of language in my classroom. Last warning: sit down, and stop disrupting my class."

"I think he's just as crazy as her."

"Shut. The fuck. Up."

"Mr. Jennings!"

Before anyone could say any more, Chloe stood up, grabbing Kal's arm, leading him out into the hallway. She shut the classroom door and slammed him against the lockers.

"What the hell do you think you're doing?" She demanded an explanation.

He gritted his teeth, "Don't act like you didn't hear them."

"Yes, I heard them, but none of it was even true."

"Exactly," he argued, "They're saying all of this—"

"So, it shouldn't bother you. It's not true, and we know it's not. So, they can say whatever—"

Kal stopped her, "No, Chloe. They *can't* say whatever. How can you sit there and—"

"I'm sorry that I have a little self control, Kal." She scoffed.

"You know what Chloe—"

She interrupted him this time, by clapping her hands, "Good job, really, *really* great."

"I'm sorry for trying to defend you, it won't happen again."

"I don't know if you're even capable of stopping, you have like a superhero complex or something." She spat.

"Guess we'll find out," he shoved away from her, steaming down the hall until the shoved the double doors open, leaving school.

Chloe just stood there for a moment, angry tears in her eyes as she asked herself aloud, "What the hell just happened?"

She left school after lunch; she couldn't take anymore of the whispers, not after the fight her and Kal had during chemistry. Taking her short walk home, a car honked at her from the curb, as if it had been sitting there waiting for her. She pretended to not see it at first, casually kneeling down and grabbing a rock to use as a weapon before she looked over at the car.

"I'll find both of you," The Gamer's voice whispered in her head, haunting her.

She held the rock tightly in her hands, slowly and carefully walking to the car.

"Please, don't leave."

"Dad," she only felt a little bit relieved, loosening her tight hold on the rock.

"You aren't planning on using that rock on *me*, are you?"

"Depends," she answered honestly, shifting her weight uncomfortably.

He looked sad, "Look, Chlo, I just wanted to tell you…that I'm sorry."

"Sorry for…what, exactly?"

"I didn't mean to do any of it. Your face, that gun, and now your mother. I'm so sorry."

Chloe's heart sank, "Mom? What'd you do to her?"

"I'm sorry, I'm *so* sorry," he cried.

Her eyes wandered from his face to his lap, where he had a shotgun that was pointed toward his chin. It was a big shotgun, one with two barrels. These next moments were as if she were racing. She left her father, turning around and sprinting at full speed, heading to her house for two main reasons. One, she couldn't be seen at *another* crime scene, not with the rumors going around about how psychotic she was; and two, she had to see her mother.

Her stomach was in her throat and her heart was on the ground as she ran. As she heard the shotgun's loud bang, the image in her head wouldn't leave; it was permanently projected out in front of her: her father's eyes, the way he didn't even seem the slightest bit scared as he held the gun to his chin.

She tore the front door open, "Mom?" She asked as she looked into the kitchen, "Mom, where are you?"

She went into the living room, tripping over the knocked over lamp, landing right next to her mother's wide-eyed corpse. Screaming, she stood up quickly, backing away with her hand over her own mouth in shock, inching toward the door. It was her only way of escape. She had to leave.

Kal opened the bathroom door, steam from the hot, complicated shower he had just taken rolling out. He dried the part of his leg where the cast and it met, so no water slipped in. He walked in just his jeans into the living room, towel-drying his hair sloppily, not really caring. The phone rang, and he answered it quickly, tossing the towel down onto a chair.

"Yeah?"

It was Anna, "Hey," she whispered, "where did you go?"

"Home," he answered dryly.

"I thought we were gonna talk. It's fifth hour," she said slowly.

"Sorry," yet the tone was anything but apologetic.

"What's with you lately, Kalvin? Ever since you got back you've been so different."

"Sorry," he repeated.

"I don't think I like it at all."

"I bet you don't." He really didn't feel like dealing with this right now.

"See? That's what I'm talking about. You're so…annoying."

"Sorry."

"No wonder Chloe left school during lunch. *You* probably set her off, didn't you?" She accused.

"Is there a point to this conversation?" He asked.

"Maybe," she hesitated.

"Maybe, what? Maybe I should hang up now because this conversation's not going anywhere? Sounds like a good idea. Bye-bye."

"Kalvin!" she yelled.

He hung up, sighing and walking toward the kitchen to get something to eat. As he opened the refrigerator, there was a loud, sudden bang on the front door. Glad his aunt was out shopping and that his uncle was out at work, he shut the refrigerator and grabbed the gun that was kept on top of it. When he reached the door, he turned the knob, pulling it open only a crack to look out and see who it was.

"Chloe," he put the gun into his pack jeans pocket, opening the door a little farther, keeping a straight face because he remembered he was mad at her, asking meanly, "What?"

She broke down, alarming him slightly. Tears streamed down her face and she sniffled, looking away, also remembering they were supposed to be mad at each other, "My...."

How was she supposed to tell him? Both of her parents had just died, both at her father's hand, but how? How would she tell him that her father had just murdered her mother and committed suicide? She couldn't believe it, it was too unreal. This wasn't her life, she has had enough problems, why would this happen to her?

Dropping the angry face quickly, he lead her into the house, closing and locking the door, asking, "What happened?" as he heard police sirens screaming,

Chloe walked numbly over to the stairs, sitting down on one, shaking slightly. He sat down next to her, gently prying the rock she still had in her clutches away from her, looking at her face, studying it, as if it would tell him what had happened.

"What happened?" he repeated.

She couldn't speak; all of her emotions were coming out with her tears, all she could do was cry. All she could feel was the numb feeling of what could only be described as an out of body and out of mind dream. A dream she couldn't wake up from.

"Okay," he said, standing up, "hold on a second."

"No," Chloe choked, grabbing his wrist.

He quickly looked down at her, kneeling down to be somewhat at her height.

"Don't leave," she pleaded.

"I'm not leaving," he promised, "I'm gonna call Becky, I'll be right back. I promise." He assured her, grabbing onto her arm.

She nodded, letting him go.

Kal quickly ran into the kitchen, grabbing the phone and dialing a number quickly, "Hey Becky, can you hurry home? I'll uh...explain later, when you get home." He hung up, then grabbed a wash-cloth and wet it down, bringing it back to Chloe. As he put it to her head, he began to pick her up.

She didn't seem as scared anymore, not with him, not while he was taking care of her. She slipped away comfortably; although some of it had to do with the amount of shock her body was in. She went into a deep sleep. There, in that dream, nothing was wrong at all.

Kal watched as Chloe's eyes fluttered closed, her neck going limp, head falling back as all of her muscles relaxed. He picked her up and carried her up the stairs to his bedroom, setting her down on the bed, placing the wet towel on her head. After that, he went swiftly down the stairs to get her a cup of water, but there was a knock on the door.

When he answered it, a policeman stood in the doorway, so he asked politely, "Can I help you, officer?"

"Are your parents home, son?"

"My aunt and uncle are gone, no."

The officer went on anyway, "Well, have you seen Chloe Johnson? I believe she's a very good friend of yours. Have you seen her today?"

"Yeah, at school." Kal answered honestly.

"We just found her father in a car not far down the road. And her mother is inside the house. They're both dead, son. I would just like to find miss Johnson. So I'm going to ask you again, have you seen her within the last half hour?"

"Do you think she killed them?" He tried to remain as calm as possible.

The policeman's eyes narrowed, "Just call if you hear from her, okay, son?"

"Sure," he went inside and shut the door, saying under his breath, "I'm not your damn son."

He waited for the cop to leave before he left the door, getting Chloe's water. As he was starting to go up the stairs, his aunt Becky came into the house, asking frantically, "Kal! What's going on? You sounded so—"

"Something's going on with Chloe. I don't know the full story, but you have to swear not to tell the cops or anything—"

"Cops? What kind of trouble are you in?"

"Becky, *please.*" He begged.

"Okay," she agreed, seeing his obvious desperation, "Where is she?"

"She's upstairs in my-" he stopped, quickly finishing the sentence, "-room." He decided that saying she was in his bed may have been a bad idea, "She passed out. I think she's just overwhelmed. When she wakes up, I'll get the story, but don't tell anyone she's here. All I know is that her parents *both* just died."

Becky nodded, frowning at the situation, "I won't say anything. Bring her up that water, and get a wet towel."

"Already on it," he thanked, running up the stairs again. He set the glass on the table and sat down in the computer chair, looking at Chloe's calm face as she slept.

He could tell she was scared or freaked out about something, because she began to mumble again, "I need to tell you...." She paused and rolled onto her side, facing him, her face snuggling into his pillow, "I have to tell you....I should've...." She trailed off.

He watched her curiously, wondering what could have been so bad that she would risk losing him to tell him? What was so important? Her eyes moved slowly in her closed sockets, and the corners of her mouth pulled into a small, sweet smile.

"Kal, I...." Her eyes snapped open and she shot up quickly, looking around.

Kal jumped, "Hey, lay back down," he felt ashamed, like he was reading her diary or something.

She obeyed, looking around, "How'd I get up here?"

"Drink this," he said quietly, holding the cup of water to her lips.

She grabbed the glass gently, her pinking and ring finger touching his warm hand, his touch distracting her slightly.

"Are you okay?" He set the glass back down on the table, sitting down on the bed by her, sitting by her hip as she was leaning against the headboard of the bed, sitting up.

She nodded, "I'm okay."

He didn't want to pressure her, "Okay."

She eyed him weakly, "No arguments?"

"Nope," he answered quietly, looking at her.

Her eyes narrowed, but she moved on, "Kal, look, I...."

"Don't, you don't have to apologize, it was me."

"But I didn't have to—"

"I was on edge, and I hated it when people talk about you like that. It drives me crazy."

"Yeah, I saw that." She added humor to the moment.

He nodded, smiling, hanging his head and looking at her puppy-eyed and cute as ever, "So *I'm* sorry, okay?"

"Can't stay mad at ya forever," she looked down, blushing and smiling uncontrollably.

He longed to ask her what happened, but he didn't want to cause her to pass out again, so he just sat and waited in silence, knowing she would tell him when she was ready.

Finally, she looked up at him, "When I left the school, my dad…he was waiting in a car on the curb and he told me…that he was sorry for everything."

He watched carefully, watching her face as it tried hiding pain.

"Well," she continued, "then he um…shot himself. He killed my Mom, Kal. When I got home she was dead. After that it's all pretty hazy, I guess I came here."

Kal nodded, informing her, "The police stopped by. I told 'em I hadn't seen you."

"Thank you," she said gratefully.

"Of course," he held out his arms for a hug, so she knelt forward.

She held him tightly, her face touching his bare shoulder, his wet hair dampening her arms, which were around his neck. He had his hands on her back, pulling her closer. She never wanted to move, freezing time would have been perfectly fine with her. Her heart seemed to momentarily be gone, it most likely left with her brain, and maybe even her stomach. She couldn't feel anything but his heartbeat. Finally, when her brain, heart, and stomach returned, she felt him start to pull away, so she kept her hands behind his neck. Maybe if she held him, he could never leave her again.

After quite a while, Kal pulled away and grabbed her hands, holding them as he lowered them from his neck, "You need to keep drinking." He handed her the glass of water again.

She took it, still feeling his hands on her back, wishing they were still there as she took a small sip.

"Are you okay? You look sick or something."

"I'm okay," she nodded, arguing with herself, *liar.*

"Okay," he kissed her forehead, momentarily stealing her breathing ability away from her.

"Does Becky know?" She asked, concerned.

"Yeah, and you're staying here whether you like it or not." He informed her, setting the glass of water back onto the table.

She rolled her eyes and grinned, laying back down and getting comfortable again, re-situating the blankets.

CHAPTER 9

After dinner, Kal left to sneak into Chloe's house and get her clothes; meanwhile, Chloe sat in Kal's room, watching TV. She flipped through the channels quickly, mind nowhere on the screen. She had been doing this same exact thing for a few minutes, and she finally decided on a channel when she heard the front door open and close.

A few minutes later, Kal came through the bedroom door with an arm full of clothes, "Here, I'm not really sure what's what. I just pulled stuff out of the dryer."

"'Kay, thanks."

He set them down on his computer desk on top of his keypad, "I guess I'll see you tomorrow." He turned to leave.

"Kal," She said quickly, a little louder than she had intended.

He turned and looked at her.

She tried to wind down, licking her lips to steady herself before she spoke, "I need to talk to you about something."

"Okay," he said in a tone that stated simply: *all you had to do was ask*, sitting down on the bed with her again.

"Okay, um…" she began, "I'm just gonna talk and you have to promise to shut up and listen, okay?" Her voice shook with nerves.

"Sure," he agreed, nodding.

"Okay," she began again, throat dry with nervousness, "Okay, remember not to say anything. Don't even make any gestures or facial expressions—"

"Chloe," he put his finger to her mouth, "I promise." When she seemed calm, he removed his hand, looking at her curiously.

His shaggy dark hair started to look more and more perfect, his blue-green eyes impossible to look into if she wanted to breathe at all for the rest of the night. All she could do was look down, speaking quietly, mouth dry, staring at her feet at she crossed her legs to try to steady her shaking as her nerves overcame her.

"I should have said something way before now," she stopped there, knowing that she had officially started the conversation, there was no going back.

"Should have said what, Chlo?"

She thought her eyes were going to burn a hold in the floor, so she refocused her gaze on a football that was lying nearby, asking, "Are you...happy?"

He cocked his head slightly, staring at her to try to convince her to look at him, "Happy?"

"With Anna, I mean," she specified, stomach churning.

He shrugged, relaxing slightly, "I guess. I mean, honestly, she's just a high school crush. I don't expect to spend my life with her or anything.

"Oh," she sounded too happy, so she added blandly, "I see."

"Are you okay?"

"Yeah," she answered quickly.

"You're just acting kinda weird. You look pale." He observed aloud.

"Yeah," Chloe said, biting her lip, "that's because I'm about to share one of my deepest darkest, yet obvious secrets with you."

He looked very interested, "What're you talking about, Chloe? We tell each other everything. No secrets."

"Well," she raised her eyebrows, breathing in deeply, "There's something major I've been keeping to myself for a long time."

"You can tell me." He convinced.

Ok. Here it goes. I don't know if I can do this…. No, you can, just tell him. If you keep it to yourself, he'll find somebody else. Tell him. She tried speaking, but the only thing that came out was, "Hmmn."

"Take your time," he encouraged in a funny tone, although she didn't laugh.

Eventually, everything just spilled out of her mouth, "Kal, I think you dating Anna is a mistake. You said it yourself, you two aren't meant for each other."

He seemed to agree, "Yeah…what's your reasoning, though?"

"That's the obvious part." She muttered, quickly moving on, "Okay, remember that time in Kindergarten when we first talked?"

"Yeah," he laughed slightly, "I got yelled at so much, I'm pretty sure it scarred me for life."

The first day of Kindergarten, everyone was excited. The teacher put everyone in assigned seats and told them, "Now remember who you're sitting by. There's a dot on your desk, can you remember what color you are?"

Chloe's dot was yellow, the girl sitting next to her had a red dot, the boy across from the girl had a green dot, and the boy across from Chloe had a blue dot.

The teacher told them to get acquainted with the people they were sitting with, and they did; after the teacher explained what acquainted meant, of course.

"I'm Casey Bryant." The red-dotted girl spoke first, smiling, one of her front teeth already missing.

"I'm Chloe, my last name is Johnson, but I don't know how to spell that yet."

"I can't spell my last name neither," the boy with the blue dot spoke up, "how do you spell Jennings?"

"I don't know," the green dot chimed in, "But I'm Aaron. There's two A's in my name, but I'm not sure why."

After while, the teacher let them do a small project, which involved markers. They were all assigned to color a picture; but, while Chloe was at a different table, asking to borrow a yellow marker for the sun in her picture, Aaron decided it would be hilarious if he drew a bit "X" on Chloe's picture, so he did. Kal and Casey didn't notice, they were too distracted by their own drawings. When Chloe came back over and saw the "X", she frowned, so Kal and Casey looked up at her.

"What's the matter?" He asked her.

"Look," she pointed to her picture as Aaron snickered.

Kal looked at Chloe's sad face, then at Aaron. He quickly grabbed a black marker, coloring all over Aaron's Power Ranger drawing.

"Hey!" Aaron yelled, shoving Kal's hand away.

"Tell her you're sorry," he demanded.

"No," Aaron refused.

Kal then put the marker to Aaron's face, drawing all over his lips and nose. When Aaron started to cry, the teacher looked over, quickly coming to see what was going on. When the situation was clear, Kal was sent away and yelled at, but not before he gave Chloe the drawing that he had made, telling her:

"You can keep it."

"I can't believe I remember that so well," Chloe said, shaking her head.

"I can. Those teachers scared me," he laughed lightly.

Chloe laughed with him, but it faded when she thought of what to say next to finish her story, "We became friends immediately," *unlike you and Anna,* "and it was just so…easy," *unlike you and Anna.*

"Yeah, it was." He agreed.

"But then…for me…things changed. A lot, actually. Around fifth grade."

"How?"

You're so stupid. "Remember your birthday?"

"Which one?"

"In fifth grade, when you were sick." She specified, trying to clear things up.

Snow day. Yes. Chloe sat on her couch, watching TV and covering up, eventually deciding to call Kal.

The phone rang twice before Kal's father answered, "Hello?"

"It's Chloe," was all she had to say.

"Hold on...Kal!"

She waited for about 30 seconds, hearing the sound of someone handling the phone before Kal finally spoke.

"Hellow?" He sounded sick.

"Hellow." She mocked him, giggling.

"I'b sick." He told her, sniffling.

"Nooo," she complained, stamping her foot.

"I amb doo. My dose is all sduffed up and dad says I have a demperdure of like a hundred and dwo," he sniffled again, sounding miserable.

"Who am I gonna spend my snow day with?"

"I dunno. Sorry, Chlo."

"Okay, get better. Talk to you later," she barely waited to hear his goodbye before she hung up, running into the kitchen.

After a while, she had a tray with two bowls of soup, spoons, and some vitamins. She had her coat, gloves, hat, and snow boots on as she went out the door, walking across the street and down a few houses to Kal's house.

Once she got there, she knocked with her foot, adjusting her had with her shoulder, hands full.

His father answered, "Chloe, hey, how ya doing?"

"I'm fine, but I heard Kal's not doing so well so I stopped by," she lifted the tray a little, smiling.

"Sure, sure, come on in," he smiled, letting her inside.

She went into the living room, seeing Kal lying on the couch, a box of Kleenexes on the table, used one strewn out all over.

"You are sick," she let herself be known, looking down at him helplessly.

"Go 'way, I'll get you sick doo." He warned.

"I brought you some breakfast," she ignored him, sitting down on the tiny edge of the couch he wasn't taking up, "And vitamins. You might want to take them as soon as possible, you look awful," she smiled widely, her braces showing.

He sat up, one overall strap unbuckled, his bowl-cut hair messy and wild.

"You look really awful," she told him.

"Danks," he sniffled, "I veel terrible."

She couldn't help but laugh at the speech problem his nose was causing him, "Oday."

He glared at her, trying to grin.

"I'm just kidding," she hugged his arm.

"Ad leasd by best friend sdopped by when I'b sick."

That was the first time in their relationship where Chloe had to fake a smile, and it bothered her. What made her so sad? As she hugged his arm, she went over the sentence he said in great scrutiny, only coming up with one reason it could have made her upset. "Best friend." That was the only explanation.

She was surprised, because she didn't choose this crush, and she wasn't ready for it, either. It snuck up on her, out of nowhere. She didn't have an option….

"Wasn't that the first time we hugged?" Kal asked.

"Yeah," Chloe remembered.

"Well, what do you mean by *things changed*?" He questioned.

"I mean…I kind of started to…like you." She looked at his face carefully, waiting for everything to go wrong.

His eyebrows twitched, but he took control of himself quickly, face smooth and straight, "Like…like a crush on me?"

She hesitated, but then nodded reluctantly, nerves crawling through her veins.

He looked away, scratching the back of his head, avoiding eye contact, "Wow, well…. Why didn't you tell me?" He finally looked at her.

"I don't know," she stood up and went into a quick pace back and forth in front of him, "I should have, and I can't believe you never noticed. I don't usually flirt with all my other friends, Kal. But, I guess it must have just not been obvious to you, because of Anna or something. But it went on for a while, and then I started to *really* like you, and then—" she stopped, slumping back down into a sitting position on the bed, "She came into the picture," she referred to Anna, knowing he would know who she meant.

"Wow," he said again, "is that why you didn't ever wanna go on our double date? You always avoided it."

"You're never gonna let me live that down, are you?" She asked.

He shook his head, adding in his charming grin.

"And I asked you not to talk till I was finished." She scolded.

"I thought you were done," he told her simply.

"Shut up," she ordered.

"Okay, okay, I'm shut."

She went on, "I mean, you can't honestly say you didn't notice any of it. It was all over the place, every day, everything we did together and...I just can't believe you honestly didn't notice." She looked at him, waiting for a response.

He sat there silently.

"No comment?"

He still sat silently.

"Are you pleading the fifth on that one?" She was getting slightly annoyed.

Still, he sat there silently, not moving a muscle.

"Hello?" she clapped twice, "can you not speak?"

"You told me not to say anything till I was done."

She glared at him, not laughing.

His smile disappeared from his face when he discovered she didn't find it funny, and he got serious again, "Okay, well, I did kind of think you were into me…at that Christmas party at my house a year ago."

"How?"

He looked at her cautiously, "I…overheard you and Aaron talking."

Chloe remembered when she used to talk to Aaron. When she thought he was her friend, but, it turned into him being obsessively in love with her. Then he tried to kill her. Now he was dead. Couldn't everything go back to a year ago?

Kal's annual Christmas party. It was always fun, but Chloe found she had butterflies in her stomach as she walked in, mistletoe hanging in every doorway. She saw Aaron walk into the kitchen, so she quickly followed.

"Aaron," she got his attention as Christmas music played from the stereo that sat in the living room.

"Hey," he handed her a drink.

"Thanks," she looked at him, "Okay, I walk thinking about some things."

"Yeah?" He asked, taking a drink of his eggnog.

"Yeah, and it would be totally cool if you like…talked to Kal for me."

"About you?"

"No!" she yelled quickly, making him jump and slosh his drink.

"Shit," he mumbled, looking from his cup back up to Chloe, "Then what would I talk to him about?"

"I thought maybe about Anna," she said hopefully.

Kal came into the kitchen, ducking behind the counter to search the cabinets for more plastic cups.

"You want me to tell Kal that he should break up with Anna?" Aaron asked, setting his eggnog down and taking off his stained hoodie.

"No, you're right, that's stupid." She said, shaking her head and setting her cup down, too.

"I never said it was stupid," he told her.

"Just forget it," she smiled, "but thanks anyways."

"Chloe, if you like him, you should just—"

"I don't," she told him, turning around and walking out of the kitchen.

Kal stood up, cups in his hands as he walked out slowly, denial on his face; denial that took him over as the night carried on.

"Then I though that you hadn't told me anything before, sop why should I give up Anna for you? If I didn't even know if you liked me that way. I always thought you liked Aaron, that's why I always tried hooking you guys up," he confessed.

"What?" she made a face, then stopped, asking him," Were you…into me, too?"

He looked down, swallowing and saying, "I think it'd be best if I pleaded the fifth on that one," holding a serious face for a moment, but a smile followed it as he looked at her.

"Seriously," she urged, "I won't be mad. I know you probably don't see me this way, and I probably should have never brought it up, but I couldn't hold it in any longer. Not after I thought I lost you. Twice, might I add. Just please tell me the truth, 'cause—"

"Yes."

She paused, wondering if she heard correctly, "…what?"

"Yes, I felt the same way, but—"

"But now you've got a girlfriend, and you're super duper happy, yeah, yeah." She wanted to skip that part of the story.

"But," he continued, "I made a mistake in not saying anything to you first."

It was as if Chloe had forgotten how to inhale.

He went on, not liking the silence that followed, "I mean, if I woulda said something, we would have…. I mean, we could have…."

"Well now you *have* said something," she said, "and so have I. So…what now?"

There was a short silence before Kal leaned forward, tucking a strand of hair behind Chloe's ear with one finger. He leaned in closer, looking into her eyes carefully, as if he was seeing if this was okay. She responded to his silent question, leaning slowly toward him, only daring to inch so far before she stopped, looking down from Kal's eyes to his lips. They got closer, close enough to feel each other's breath on their lips. Chloe closed her eyes…waiting for the kiss she had been waiting for. Their first *real* kiss, because the one before didn't count in her mind.

"Oh!" Becky's voice was full of surprise.

Kal stood up quickly, stumbling slightly off of the bed, looking at his aunt, who was standing in the doorway, "Becky."

"I'm sorry, I didn't realize you two were—"

"No," Kal shook his head, "No, no. That…no. Nothing was happening."

"You weren't…?"

"No," he answered quickly, putting his hands into his jeans pocket.

"Why don't you come downstairs, Kal," Becky said in a motherly tone.

He scratched his neck awkwardly, glancing for only a moment at Chloe before he quickly walked out, not looking back as his aunt followed him, closing the bedroom door behind them.

Chloe sighed loudly and laid down, slamming her head into the pillow as she stared up at the ceiling. She ran her fingers through her dirty blonde hair, crawling under the covers and snuggling into the bed. The scent of Kal would be enough for now, but right now she loathed Becky. Becky stole him away, only a few seconds before the moment she had wished for since the fifth grade. But still, she wondered why Kal was going to kiss her in the first place. He had Anna, would he really cheat on her just because he could? What he *that* kind of guy?

She took her mind off of that, wondering if Kal was planning on going to school tomorrow. She didn't really care; if they went, it wasn't like they would stay too long without someone yelling. By someone, she knew it would be Kal. All she knew what that things were never going to be the same, and the Gamer was still out there waiting. Waiting to find her and Kal.

This was a fact that was abruptly proven the next morning.

CHAPTER 10

"Chloe!" Kal yelled, waking her up as he burst through the bedroom door, "You have to see this," he turned on the TV that was in his room, flipping quickly to the right channel.

The broadcaster said, "…were found earlier this morning, tied to a streetlight pole. The word GAMER was burned and cut into their chests, like the other Gamer victims, but what was different about these two victims is what was branded on their *backs*."

Kal looked at Chloe, watching her instead of the TV.

The broadcaster went on without emotion, as usual, "The message said, and I quote, '*You two better be ready, because I'm getting close*'. Police are clueless as to who this Gamer could be, but they are watching the two escaped victims carefully, and they are doing their best to keep their eyes out. If you know anything pertaining to the Gamer, please give them a call—"

Kal turned off the TV, looking at Chloe for a response.

"That didn't exactly say morning sunshine," she groaned, still half asleep, yawning.

"He wants us to know he's coming for us, and soon."

"We already knew that, Kal. He's just trying to scare us to make it fun. He likes *games*, remember?" She stayed considerably calm.

"He's not trying to scare us, he is scaring us."

"Are you kidding me?"

He shook his head.

She looked at him as if he were a little boy, explaining, "He's just trying to freak us out, he's toying with us. If we stay level-headed, we can outsmart him and he won't be able to win the game he's playing."

"Chloe. Who stays level-headed in these kinda situations?" He demanded, "This isn't a movie."

"Kal," she kept her voice firm, "Either we kill, or we get killed. That's how this is going to end, whether we like it or not."

He looked down, as if that thought hadn't come to his mind at all, like it was hitting him for the first time. After the longest pause, he finally said, "When you put it that way...."

"Breakfast!" Becky yelled.

Ever since their encounter in Kal's bedroom, she never let them be in there alone for too long. She always found some excuse to make one of them come down, being the nervous substitute mother that she needed to be.

When they got down the stairs, there was a tap on the door, so Becky went to answer it as Kal and Chloe grabbed a plate, looking at the pans of food. As the door opened, Kal was scooping scrambled eggs onto Chloe's plate, whispering in her ear about how paranoid they had made Becky.

"Hi, Kalvin," Anna came into the house, looking from Chloe to Kal, her mouth in a straight line.

There was a tense silence, where everyone paused, as if time froze. Becky shut the door, "Err...you want some breakfast, Anna?"

"No thank you," she looked at Chloe, "The police came to my house. They told me they were looking for you. They said to call if I...."

Chloe glanced at Kal, a worried look on her face.

Anna spoke again, "I won't say anything. You saved my life, it's the least I can do; and I know you haven't done anything wrong. Whatever they're looking for you for, I know you didn't do it. But...why are you *here*?"

"She had nowhere else to stay," Kal explained dryly.

Anna nodded, nodding toward the living room, "Kalvin, we need to talk."

"Yes." He agreed, "We do." He went first, leading the way.

As they went into the living room, Becky took Kal's plate and set it down on the table, motioning for Chloe to do the same. She sat down, no longer hungry, catching a few words here-and-there from Kal and Anna.

"Why...so early?" Anna whispered.

"...sleep here...police."

"...your bedroom!"

"....couch," he argued.

"Right, because when I slept over, you slept on the couch." She whispered louder, probably so Chloe could hear, *"And* nothing *happened, right?"*

"You know what, I'm sick of this, you—"

"....Chloe," Anna spat her name.

Chloe and Becky looked at each other, then looked down at their plates of untouched food.

Kal whispered, *"...you may think...through a lot...no idea."*

"So you're just gonna run off with your cute little blonde and think that everything will be okay? Think, for once in your life, Kalvin."

Kal was no longer whispering, "It's our only option. We have to."

"There's no safer way?"

It didn't sound like they were arguing anymore, so Chloe peeked over, trying to see them.

"Be careful," she kissed his cheek, staring up at him, crossing her arms, "Goodbye."

He didn't move as he watched her walk out of the front door before he went into the kitchen with Chloe and Becky, sitting down in his chair. He ate a few pieces of bacon before he finally looked up at them and spoke, relieving Chloe's fears, "She won't tell anyone."

"What was that all about?" Becky asked, "Who was that?"

"That was my ex."

Ex!? Chloe almost choked on the eggs she had just spooned into her mouth.

"We broke up the other day at school. She's just worried. She saw the news."

"Oh," Becky nodded, looking at Chloe, who was suddenly very interested in her scrambled eggs, "are you two going to school today?"

Chloe wasn't listening. She was too deep in thought: Kal and Anna broke up at school, which meant that he had been single the entire time she had been there with him, he wasn't going to cheat on Anna at all. He was actually a good guy, sincerely.

Kal answered after Chloe didn't, "I don't know. We were thinking about going out, actually."

She choked on her eggs, for real this time, at the words "going out". He handed her a drink, so she quickly tried gulping some down.

"Where were you going?" Becky asked, patting Chloe on the back, concerned.

Kal eyed Chloe, also concerned as he went back to the conversation; "Um…" then he changed his sentence, looking at a still-choking Chloe again, "are you alright?"

Her choking slowed, but she was still coughing, eyes watering as her throat burned, "Yeah," she croaked, taking another drink.

Kal answered Becky, "We just need to get our minds off of things."

"Okay, just don't get into any trouble," she warned with many meanings, walking into the living room, leaving them alone. Of course, she was still at a close enough distance to keep somewhat of an eye on them.

"Are you sure you're okay?" He looked at her beat-red face and watery eyes.

She nodded, taking a drink, "I think I'm good now."

"Good. I just thought we'd get out of here for a while so we can clear our heads," he picked up his plate, setting it on the counter, grabbing the keys to his truck, "After you're done, go get dressed, and I'll meet you out there, okay?"

She nodded, chancing another bite of eggs.

"Don't die while I'm gone."

"I'll do my best."

Kal grinned opening the door. Almost as quickly as his grin faltered, he was back inside with the door closed, the yelling that boomed stopping with the slam of the door.

"What's wrong?" Chloe sat up straighter.

"Cameras, microphones, and yelling reporters. Stupid yelling reporters." He grumbled.

"Great."

"I'll wait for you to get ready and we'll head out at the same time."

She nodded, quickly finishing her plate, rinsing it off before running up the stairs to find some clothes. She decided on jeans and a light brown spaghetti-strap that Kal had once complimented her on, brushing through her hair with Becky's brush as she did her makeup. After she thought she looked presentable enough, she hurried downstairs, grabbing her white hooded jacket Kal had brought over for her.

"Ready for this?" Kal asked as he watched her come down the stairs.

"Not really," she replied, putting her jacket on and joining him by the door, but she couldn't help but wonder if he was checking her out as he looked down at her.

"Me neither," he sighed as he put his arm around her upper back, hugging her close as he opened the door, leading her out, protecting her from the savage crowd.

They were swarmed by dozens of reporters, their microphones automatically zooming toward their faces. Questions buzzed loudly, colliding together, barely comprehendible.

"Kalvin! Do you think the Gamer will find you?"

"Kalvin! What was it like, being an escaped victim of the Gamer?"

"Kalvin! Any comments on the victims found—"

"Chloe! Chloe!" They finally noticed that she was there, too.

"How do you feel about this?"

"Any ideas on who the Gamer is?"

"Did you see his face?"

"Break it up," a police car pulled up, "Go on, now! They're just kids, for God's sake. Let them through."

The crowd slowly cleared up as the police officer shook his head, walking up to Kal and shaking his hand, "I'm officer Hemingway. Would you like a ride to school?"

Kal jingled his keys, "Thanks, officer, but I think we're okay."

Hemingway nodded his bald head, then went back to his car as Kal opened the passenger's side door of the truck for Chloe, who hopped in as he ran around, getting in the driver's side.

"Kal...." Chloe whispered, looking at the rearview mirror, which had what they sincerely hoped was red paint. The red liquid was dried now, but it spelled out a word that made each of their stomachs ache.

GAMER.

Kal quickly looked in the back seats, but there was nobody there. They looked at each other, holding their breath with fear.... The sound of Chloe's phone ringing made them both jump, and she closed her eyes as she answered.

"Hello?"

"Hello, Chloe." The Gamer's deep voice rumbled in her ear.

She looked around, swallowing, "Where are you? What do you want?"

Kal shut the truck door, locking both of them before he started the truck, grabbing the wheel and looking at Chloe for a sign of what to do.

"You will do exactly as I say, or Kal will die. Understand?"

Chloe looked at Kal, shutting her mouth.

"What's going on?" He asked, clenching his jaw.

"Don't tell him anything," the Gamer ordered, "just trust that I can kill Kal if you slip up. Right now, I could kill him. Tell him to drive."

Chloe hesitated, looking out of the windows again.

"Tell him to drive," he repeated coldly.

"Chloe, what?" Kal asked.

"Drive." She said dryly.

"What?"

"Drive," she repeated, looking into his eyes sharply, lips tight together in desperation.

"This is crazy," he said, gently pushing on the gas pedal.

"Go right."

"Turn right," Chloe relayed.

"Chloe—"

"Kal, please." She begged.

"Open the glove compartment, you will find a CD. I'd like for you to put it in and listen to it. Don't turn it off," he laughed at his game moves, he was obviously proud of them, "And Chloe, don't fuck up."

She put the phone down after pressing "end", and then she opened the glove compartment, finding the CD, taking it out of it's case.

"What's that?" Kal asked, worried.

She put the CD in, "We have to do what he says. He wants us to listen to this." She pushed play.

First, it was the Gamer's voice that played, instructing them to look under the seat for a map. There was a route marked, and they needed to follow it. After his instructions, the song "Highway to Hell" by ACDC began to play.

Kal and Chloe looked at each other.

This was definitely proof that the Gamer loved playing his game.

"I think it's a left up ahead," Chloe said, squinting, confused at the map.

"We're venturing out to nowhere," Kal argued, "and Highway to Hell is on repeat because the damn thing won't come out of the CD player."

"Kal, he told me something about you, and he told me I can't tell you about—"

As she was speaking, her phone rang again, so she snapped her mouth shut.

"Can he hear us?"

Chloe answered the phone, putting it to her ear, not making a sound.

"I can see you, I can hear you. I control you. You're just my pawns that are in my way in a very important game of chess, so stop trying to be smart, because I will kill you faster than you can think about running away, do you understand?" Before she could answer, he hung up.

In anger, Chloe closed her phone and slammed it onto the dash. Then she looked at it, seeing the cracked screen, mumbling, "Dammit," before throwing it out of the window, hoping he couldn't reach them anymore.

The chorus of the song chimed again, "Highway to Hell! We're on a highway to Hell!"

Kal's cell phone rang this time, so Chloe took it out of his pocket and answered it, "Hello?"

"Nice move, throwing your phone out the window," he sounded bored, "Good thing I'm not trigger happy or your lover would be all over the inside of that car."

All over? That sounds more like a bomb to me, she thought, answering him, "It broke."

"Just all of a sudden? Poof, broken phone? Nice try."

"No, I slammed it down 'cause you piss me off." She answered honestly.

He laughed, giving her chills again, instructing, "Stop the truck."

"What?" she asked, looking at the map, "We aren't where you told us to go."

"Stop the truck," he repeated right before the dial tone buzzed in her ear.

"Stop the truck," Chloe relayed to Kal again.

He stepped on the brakes without question, then they both sat in silence for the longest time, just waiting for something to happen.

Finally, Kal spoke, "So are you gonna tell me what the hell's going on?"

She had to quickly change the subject, for Kal's own good, "When did you and Anna break up, again?"

He sighed, sensing her panic at his question, so he just answered hers, "School. Before school, we started talking and we agreed breaking up would be the best thing to do."

Chloe couldn't help but to think back. This new information meant, that from the moment Kal went into the gym with her, he was single. *Holy crap.* Now she was kicking herself, wishing something had actually happened between them, instead of an almost-kiss. There was a long silence as they sat in nervous anticipation, Chloe's mind racing elsewhere.

She couldn't take it anymore, she had to bring it up. After all, they might die soon, so what did she have to lose? "So last night...when you almost kissed me," she paused, but there were no objections, she went on, "what exactly...was it?" She finished, looking at him carefully, wondering if he understood her question.

He made it very clear that he understood as he leaned toward her, pausing when his face was an inch from hers. Again, it was like he was asking her for permission, but she didn't hesitate this time. She moved toward him quickly, kissing him and closing her eyes to soak in the moment. Her arms weren't stuck this time either; she put her fingers in his hair, never wanting to let him go. Not now, not now that she had him. He slid his fingers up her arm, giving her goose bumps as his hands touched her face. He kept kissing her, making up for everything he recently realized he had done to her.

He pulled away slowly, lips still an inch from hers, "I'm sorry."

She moved to kiss him again, but he stopped her, backing away a little.

"Wait."

144

"Kal, I've been waiting," her voice came out in a small whisper.

"I'm sorry," he repeated, "I'm sorry for hurting you like that."

"It's okay," she assured him, just wanting to kiss him again.

"No, it's not," she shook his head, "you should've like…hit me or something."

"Really, it's okay."

"I'll do whatever I can to make sure nobody hurts you again. I promise."

"Well, kissing was helping."

He laughed and looked into her eyes, leaning in to kiss her again, but a light shined onto his face, making them both panic slightly.

The policeman yelled into the car, "You two are being hunted by the Gamer and you drove all the way out here to make out? Really?"

"Oh crap."

"Get down!" Kal warned, knowing what was about to happen, but he was too late.

There was the sound of a silenced gunshot, then blood sprayed the truck window as the policeman fell to the ground, a bullet hole in his head. Almost immediately, Kal opened his door, jumping out and reaching back in for Chloe. When she was out, he took the gun he kept under the seat.

"Officer down!" The voice of the officer's partner yelled from somewhere Kal and Chloe couldn't see, "Officer down, we need back—" Gunshot. Thud. Silence.

"You're a good dog, Chloe. Good *bitch*."

Kal cocked the gun, rain starting to slowly sprinkle down from the clouds, dampening their hair and clothes.

"Come out, come out!" The Gamer yelled, laughing over the sound of the rain that gradually started to come down harder.

"One shot," Kal mumbled, so quiet that Chloe barely heard him, "that's all a need. One shot. Come on."

Chloe glanced under the car at the running cop car; luckily, the car was on the road, ready to drive. If only they could get to it, but she knew that chances of getting to the car alive were slim to none. The Gamer had them, now there was no getting away. This wasn't about kidnapping anymore, this was exactly as they both knew that it was. This was a game of life and death. Kill or be killed. As long as both sides were still alive, the Gamer would continue playing his game. It was like they were all just fighting dogs: they were being forced to fight till the death, however wrong or right they have to be to each other.

Chloe looked at Kal, who looked back at her. They both knew what they were going to have to do, and their faces were grim as he took her hand, the rain soaking their clothes and hair now. This was it. This was the beginning of what they knew had to be the Gamer's end. It was either the Gamer, or them.

CHAPTER 11

The Gamer taunted them, "Hey Kalvin, you prolly already got that gun out from under your truck seat, huh?" He laughed again, enjoying his role, "I gotta say, I'm not threatened."

Kal examined the gun, seeing there was no clip, which meant no bullets. He muttered and mouthed a few choice words, then set the gun down onto the truck seat, turning to Chloe.

"No bullets?"

"We have to run for it," he told her, hand still holding hers tightly.

"Your leg," she argued.

"You have to go, I'll distract—"

There was no way she was going to let him finish that sentence, "Kal, shut up. You don't need to be the hero. The hero dies in the end."

He looked at her and imagined what his life would be like without her. He didn't see her as his small crush who just so happened to be his best friend, or the girl he survived high school with. He saw her as the most amazing girl he would ever know, his best friend in the entire world, the girl nobody would ever be able to replace, not even in a million years. He saw her as the girl who would die for him, the girl who loved him. The girl who would rather die *with* him than use him as bait so she could get away and live the rest of her life. But he did *not* see her as the girl he would let run out to get packed full of bullets. There had to be a different way.

The Gamer yelled, "I got it, both of you pick a number between one and ten. We'll see who I kill first, fair and square."

Kal peeked under the car at the Gamer's feet, which were getting closer, "Chloe," he turned toward her, "I need to distract him."

"You aren't listening to me," she spoke clearly, "no."

He looked around, "Just trust me. I promise: I'll get into that police car with you, you just have to trust me."

"But—"

He didn't let her object any further. He kissed her and she stopped talking altogether. After the kiss, he got up, grabbing the gun from the truck seat, getting out from behind the truck before Chloe could stop him.

"Ah, Kal. I figured you'd be the one out first."

He aimed the empty pistol at the Gamer, making him laugh,

"You didn't count on me having an extra clip in between the seats, did you?" He lied, hoping it would work.

The Gamer's smile faltered, but then he stared, trying to read Kal's face.

"I have a question for you," Kal wiped his forehead with his shoulder, getting the wetness from his hair to stop dripping into his eyes, "Why drag Aaron into this if you were just gonna kill him?"

Once again, the Gamer laughed, "Chloe's psychotic Dad came upon my game. He said he wanted Chloe to trust him again. So, he told me to kidnap Chloe and let him save her, and only her."

Kal looked back at Chloe, who was frozen behind the truck, letting the information sink in.

The Gamer went on, "So I made Hitchson try to play the game with me...but he was so amateur. Then, her father told me he wanted to drop the whole deal. But I told him, if he wanted to do that, he'd have to find me a partner to replace him with. Even though I don't need one, that was the deal. So he found Aaron, and you know the story from there. Now," he shot his gun into the air, "you shoot yours. If it really has bullets, we'll both find out. Then we can move from their."

Kal's expression didn't change at all as he asked, "Scared?"

The Gamer shrugged, "More cautious."

Chloe made her way around the truck and started heading toward the cop car as Kal raised his gun and aimed it at the sky, a fake smirk on his face.

"Why don't I just put it to your head and pull it? Then we'll see if I'm lying."

His eyes narrowed as he looked from Kal to Chloe, analyzing the situation.

Chloe went into a quick sprint to the car, jumping in and immediately looking around for a spare gun. She found three spare clips in the glove compartment and she quickly slipped them into her pocket; then, she grabbed a gun that was left on the dash, thinking to herself, *all of the cops in this town need to be fired.* Then she rushed to take the keys out of the ignition, putting them into her pocket as well.

"Just shoot into the sky. Unless you're scared." He smiled slyly, eyes boring into Kal's as he stared him down. "I always win my game, Kalvin. Shoot. I dare you."

"How 'bout me?" Chloe asked from directly behind the Gamer.

He turned to see Chloe's gun aimed in his face.

She quickly tossed Kal one of the spare clips, locking eyes with the Gamer, telling him, "Looks like its two against one now."

The Gamer nodded, "But see…you don't have the blood of a killer flowing through you, sweet little Chloe Johnson. You can't kill, or else we wouldn't be standing here right now."

"You know nothing about me," she warned, shaking her head, holding the gun with both hands now.

"Don't I?"

"No, you don't. My Dad killed my Mom. How's that for blood of a killer?"

"Then prove me wrong, pull the trigger. Right now, free shot." He encouraged, looking at her face calmly, "Do it."

Police sirens rang in the distance, making the Gamer's head snap up, looking at the street. Kal looked at Chloe, puzzled, as the Gamer's eyes widened.

Chloe sneered, "I may not be trigger happy, but I do know how to work the radio in a cop car."

He started to run, but Kal shot him in the thigh, coming closer to his fallen body, "I'm the one that's trigger happy, bitch." He shot the Gamer's hand, leaving what looked like hamburger on the end of his arm. "And just so we're clear," he slammed the gun into the Gamer's face, snarling, "Chloe's *not* a bitch."

Chloe took the Gamer's gun and threw it far enough away, then hugged Kal, keeping her eye on the bleeding, pained Gamer as the cop cars screeched to a halt, police swarming, guns drawn at the body on the ground.

"Are you two alright?" Hemingway put his hand on Kal's shoulder as two other cops were picking the Gamer up off of the ground.

Kal nodded as Chloe rested her head on his chest.

"It's okay now," Hemingway assured, "we got him."

Neither of them were fully listening; they were both staring at the Gamer, who was getting into the back of a police car. He stared back, fury in his eyes.

"Looks like you two beat him at his own game."

ONE WEEK LATER:

Chloe and Kal sat in Kal's truck in the school parking lot. It was time for things to get back on track. The Gamer was in jail, so the story was over. Still, they sat there in silence, looking out at the people who hadn't yet noticed they were there, knowing that there would still be staring. There would still be whispers. But, eventually, it will stop, letting everyone's lives go on.

As if they read each other's minds, they both opened their doors at the same time, getting out slowly, reluctantly. Their doors closed, making a few people look over at them, Anna being one of them. She mumbled something to her group of friends she was with, securing her purse on her shoulder before making her way toward them.

"Hey, I'm so glad you two are okay," she pulled them both into a hug, "I saw the news. He's caught, right? For good?"

They all pulled out of the hug, Kal answering, "Yeah, he's gone. It's over."

Ashton, the former "school bully", walked up awkwardly, avoiding eye contact with the three, "You two... Ya know, if anyone gives you any trouble just...let me know. I'll take care of it so you don't have to," he glanced at Kal, grinning.

Kal and Chloe gave each other the same look, looking back at Ashton.

He covered up his niceness, as he turned to walk away, "See you around, love birds."

In chemistry, there were whispers at the beginning of class, but they quickly vanished when Kal stood up to "get a Kleenex", as he told the teacher. When he sat back down, he grinned menacingly at Chloe, who rolled her eyes and grinned back, resting her head on her hand, facing him slightly. Their chairs were much closer today, and he grabbed her other hand under the table, still grinning at her.

"You may begin," the teacher said.

"Begin what?" Kal whispered to her.

"Um...." She laughed, grabbing the tools she was fairly sure they needed for the assignment she was fairly sure she understood.

It was almost the end of the day, and Chloe didn't have any of her last few classes with Kal; but, to her surprise, the whispers were quiet, like less people were doing it now. She found it easy to ignore them as she worked on her history assignment, almost carefree.

The office rang in from the speakers in the ceiling, "Sorry to bother you, Mr. Wallace, but I need to speak to Chloe Johnson."

The whole class looked over at her, but she just looked at Mr. Wallace, who nodded toward the door. She got up and tucked her hair behind her ears as she avoided looking at anyone else, quickly walking out of the door.

As she walked out, she heard Mr. Wallace say to the class, "Get busy on your assignments and mind your own business."

She went into the office, seeing Kal already sitting in a chair. The councilor was standing in the corner of the room, a police officer in the other corner, as the principal sat at his desk.

"What's going on?" She questioned, looking at Kal.

He shrugged so she carefully took a seat next to him, looking up at the three adults.

"Kal, Chloe," the principal greeted them after they were both still, "We discussed it and...we think it's only fair that we tell you in person before it gets around."

Kal waited for the bell to ring to ask quietly, "Tell us what?" He locked his hands together in anticipation.

"We're dismissing school two hours early today, we're announcing it right after the kids get to their classes."

The councilor told them what they had been waiting to hear, and what the principal was postponing saying for as long as he could, "The Gamer has escaped."

Those words were like a hard, angry punch in the mouth.

Kal was on his feet now, "What? How!?" He demanded.

"The security—" The principal stopped as there was a loud bang, a pulled hole through his head as blood sprayed the councilor and police officer.

The officer drew his gun, but it was too late, he was sprayed with bullets from a bigger automatic gun, taking the counselor out, too. Kal pulled Chloe out of the seat, putting her behind him, blocking her with his own body.

The Gamer poked his head into the room, looking at them with crazed eyes, "Babies, I'm home."

He held up his machine gun for them both to see, then he aimed it at the hallway, shooting wildly, swinging the gun around everywhere, students falling to the floor, bullet holes or not. After he was satisfied with what he done, he turned back to Chloe and Kal, the new silence ringing in their ears.

"Game over, kids." He pulled the trigger.

Chloe jumped awake, looking down at her body for bullet holes, breathing heavily. The whole history class was looking at her, so she swallowed and looked down at her open book, blushing and picking her pencil up off of the floor. She felt cold sweat on her forehead, chills still spiraling up and down her spine as she wrote her name on her blank history assignment with a shaky hand.

It was only a dream. The Gamer hadn't escaped, everything was okay. The fact that the whole class now thought that she was mentally messed up didn't bother her. Perhaps she was, but at least she had the comfort of knowing that the man who made her that way was behind bars.

The rest of the day went on normally, with a few whispers and stares. In her relief, she saw Kal waiting for her at her locker after the last class of the day, with his bag on his shoulder and a grin on his face.

"Hey you."

"Hi," she smiled, getting into her locker and putting her books away as he held her locker door, peeking in.

"Your locker's so neat."

"That's because I don't have any pop cans, pop bottles, old papers, food wrappers, or any other junk you throw into yours," she teased, backing away from her locker.

He shut it for her, holding his arm out for her to take, clearing his throat and looking down at her with a charming smile. She laughed, taking his arm and letting him walk her outside to the truck.

"So how were the hours without me to scare the hell out of anyone who bothered you?" He asked as he drove them out of the parking lot.

"Well I fell asleep and had another bad dream, so when I woke up everybody was staring at me. I probably made them think I was a total loser."

"More than usual?" He teased.

"Oh shut up."

He laughed, "I was joking. You're not a loser. Straight A's just makes you a nerd, not a loser."

"If it wasn't for my straight A's, *you* wouldn't even be pulling B's and C's, mister." She warned.

"Okay, okay." He gave up, smiling to himself as he went past the old stop sign he would usually turn at.

Now that him and Chloe were staying with his aunt and uncle, the drive to and from school was only ten minutes longer than it used to be, but he still felt like he was going so far away when he passed the sign; like he was entering a whole new life entirely. In a way, he was entering a new life. This life was different than it used to be, way different. The Gamer made sure of that.

When they got there, Kal parked in the driveway, grabbing Chloe's backpack for her, putting his on his back as he got out.

"Ya know," Chloe commented, getting out, too, "I am perfectly capable of carrying my own stuff, Kal."

"I know," he said, opening the door with his other hand, "but so am I."

"Hey, kids, how was your day?" Kal's uncle Allen asked from his seat on the couch.

"We survived," Kal answered, meaning it in more than one way, feeling that he needed to announce that now.

156

"Where's Becky?" Chloe asked, grabbing her backpack from Kal and putting it on her shoulder.

"She had to work, someone called in sick," Allen answered, focusing his attention on the TV again.

"C'mon," Kal said to Chloe, leading the way up to his room to put their back packs away.

She followed him up the stairs, tossing her bag onto the floor inside the door as they went into his room.

"Finally," Kal fell into his bed, feet hanging off the edge.

"Tired?"

"Exhausted."

She stood there, crossing her arms, not really knowing what to say now.

"Hey," he looked up at her, "rock paper scissors to see who gets the bed tonight. The other takes the couch."

"Kal, you know you always lose at rock paper—"

"Just do it, I've been practicing."

That night, Chloe curled up in the bed, turning out the light as Kal went to sleep on the couch downstairs.

The next morning, there was a light tap on her door. Being the light sleeper that she was, she woke up to it, croaking, "Come in."

Kal opened the door, shirtless, she noticed, "Hey," he said, opening a dresser drawer, taking out a shirt without much deliberation. His hair was wet, he probably forgot to get a shirt when he got into the shower. She definitely didn't mind.

"Are we um…" she looked up at his face as he turned to face her, "are we going to school?"

"It's up to me now?" He questioned, slipping his shirt on over his head.

She nodded, distracting herself with a yawn.

"Hmm," he said, diving onto the bed, burying his head in the pillow next to her, mumbling something.

"What?" She asked.

He mumbled again, but the pillow made it just as inaudible as the last time.

"Huh?" She asked again, laughing.

He lifted his head up from the pillow, looking at her with messy, wet hair, "I said: it's up. To. You."

"Oh. Kay." She laughed, lying her head down on her pillow.

He grabbed the covers and threw them over both him and her, so they were completely under them, suggesting, "We could stay home."

She replied in the darkness, "We could. But what would we do?" She bit her lip, glad he couldn't see her as she blushed, "We could also go eat breakfast."

"We could," he agreed, flinging the covers off of them.

Chloe got up, but Kal got up too and pushed her back down, kissing her, "Hold on," he kissed her again,

"Kay, we can go now." He got up and pulled her up, grabbing her hand.

Smiling, and guessing she looked like a total dork, she held his hand as he lead her out the door and down the stairs into the kitchen. She felt as if she were floating, but that feeling had been around for a while now, she was used to it. It would never get old.

"Morning, Chloe," Becky said sweetly as they walked in, hands still locked together.

"Yeah, mornin'." Allen said from over his newspaper.

"Morning," Chloe answered as Kal pulled out a chair for her, "thank you," she told him absentmindedly, smiling up at him.

"No problem, bed-head." He smiled and sat down on the other side of the table, looking above her eyes at her messy hair.

She roughed-up her hair even more by running her fingers through it everywhere.

"All better," Kal chuckled, looking away.

She laughed, fixing it for real this time, brushing the tangles out with her fingers.

Words from the TV caught their attention: "...Gamer was arrested after what appeared to be a shootout. Two policemen also lost their lives in the attempt to catch him. He was identified as Milan Penn, the same man who had called himself the Driver in 1992.

"The Driver was said to have died when his car rolled during his final drive-by. Now we have captured the

Gamer and he is behind bars. The cops say he will most certainly be facing life in prison, if not the death penalty. Now over to Daryl with sports."

CHAPTER 12

"I'm goin' to work," Allen kissed Becky on the cheek, looking at the room, "See you tonight."

"Bye," Kal stated as Chloe waved.

"I better get goin' too," Becky looked at the clock that hung on the wall, "Hospital shift again. Bye bye," she kissed the top of Kal's head, warning, "Be good."

"Yeah, yeah, we will," Kal said, slightly annoyed.

"See you two later."

"Bye," Kal and Chloe said together.

After the door closed, Kal asked, "So are we going to school?"

"I asked you that."

"Yeah, but it's up to you."

"Not today," she argued, "'cause I asked you first."

"So," he replied, "I said it was up. To. You. Remember?" He bit his biscuit in half.

"Yes, I remember." She shook her head at him.

"Well, then it's your decision."

Before she could argue, the phone rang, causing them both to jump.

"She probably forgot her keys," he mumbled, standing up and picking the phone up off of the counter, answering it calmly, already looking around the counter for the keys, "Hello?"

Silence.

"Hello?" Kal repeated.

More silence.

"Don't you have caller ID?" Chloe asked him, looking up curiously from her plate of food.

He shook his head, then he quickly refocused his attention to the phone, as if someone started talking on the other end.

"You didn't think I'd be prepared for this, Kalvin?" The Gamer laughed, "Come into the garage."

Click; dial tone.

He set the phone down numbly, looking at Chloe with a blank, shocked face.

"What?" Chloe asked at his ghostly expression as she stood up, stepping toward him.

His eyes slowly moved from hers to the garage door, swallowing. She followed his gaze, looking back from the garage door to him, shaking her head wearily.

"Kal, what?"

Tap-tap...tap-tap...tap-tap-tap.

"Go outside," Kal mouthed, motioning for her to come closer to him as he grabbed the doorknob.

Tap-tap...tap-tap...tap-tap-tap.

Kal slowly turned the knob and opened the door. Even their skin was on edge as they slowly and carefully snuck out, pulling the door shut behind them. As the door shut, the Gamer's big, bulky body glided swiftly out of the garage, and there he stood, in the oil-stained driveway, a smirk on his grim and bloody face, his stubble dirty.

Kal quickly shoved Chloe back inside, rushing in behind her and slamming the door closed, locking it with shaky hands, instructing to Chloe, "Make sure the garage door is locked!"

She was already doing so as he began his sentence, securing it carefully, backing away from it.

"Go into my room," he told her as he peeked out of the peephole, "Hurry, I'm right behind you," he assured her as he ripped open the gun cabinet.

Chloe nodded and rushed up the stairs, going into Kal's room, immediately starting a search for her bag, where she had purposefully stashed two butcher knives, a pocket knife, a Taser, and one of Kal's small guns he had given her days before for protection. She unzipped it roughly and took out the pocket knife, putting it into her back pocket. The gun was simply tucked into the hip of her pants, pulling her shirt over it to hide it from sight; then, she tucked one knife under the mattress of the bed, leaving it there for easy access if all else failed. The other butcher knife was in her hand, and she was ready to use it. When she was through getting prepared, she looked up, seeing that Kal wasn't there with her yet. Something must have happened.

With shaky breaths she asked, "Kal?"

Bracing herself for the worst, she peeked out of the door, going slowly down the stairs. The house sounded dead; empty; cold; but, the walls crawled wand the ceiling wiggled with life as she made her way down one step at a time. She kept trailing down the stairs, taking the gun out and putting her finger gently on the trigger, knife in the other hand.

"Kal?" Her voice rippled through the empty, silent house.

She finally reached the bottom of the stairs, scanning the living room, and then she turned to peek into the kitchen. But, before she could look, two hands grabbed her from behind, one covering her mouth, the other grabbing the wrist of the hand that held the gun.

The Gamer whispered to her in her ear, "Time for you to lose the game, Chlo."

She tried to fight back, but he pushed her face-first into the wall, then grabbed her hair and pulled her back, slamming her forward into the wall again, making her lose her grip on consciousness....

She opened her eyes quickly, as if she were awakening from a nightmare. She wished it was a nightmare, but there was no waking up from this. This was her life. She tried to feel her head to see if there was any blood, but she couldn't move her hands; they were tied behind her hands because it was tied to a chair behind her back. Looking down at her feet, she noticed they were each tied to a chair leg. Failing miserably, she tried kicking free, but the ropes didn't budge.

Looking around, she realized what the husky, old smell was. She was in the basement, and a naked bulb in the middle of the ceiling was her only source of light as she looked across from her. Only about six feet away, Kal was tied to a chair, too.

"Kal," she said hoarsely, trying to wake him up.

Her face throbbed, her eyebrow seared with pain, burned from hitting the wall.

"Kal," she said again, voice stronger.

He stirred, then opened his eyes, looking around with droopy eyes. Finally, his eyes locked to hers.

"What happened?" She asked him, speaking slowly so he could hear her.

"I…." He shook the dazed feeling out of his head, "I got the gun out and I noticed…the lamp was off the table."

That spoke for itself, he didn't need to go on. They both wiggled around in their chairs, trying to get free. Needless to say, the only things they *did* get were rope-burned wrists. Light flooded into the basement quickly as the door creaked slowly open, the Gamer coming down with a box. He set the box down on the floor and opened it, taking out a large roll of silver duct tape, pulling some out. Tearing it with his teeth, he gently placed it over the reluctant mouths of Kal and Chloe.

He informed them, "You two can scream all you want," the deep voice echoed quietly in the musky room, "I got the TV on in the living room…." He tossed the duct tape back into the box, "There's music on upstairs. The basement doors are closed and locked. So, go right on ahead and scream."

Silence.

They didn't take the useless invitation.

"Okay, then, let's get started," he rubbed his hands together with joy, looking at the two of them, eyes hungry.

He knelt down and rummaged through his box, pulling out his lighter and a metal stick.

"No," Kal knew what those tools were used for, so he pleaded, barely understandable through the duct tape.

The Gamer flicked a couple of times on the lighter before the flame grew, licking the pole until it was red-hot, moving the lighter so the flame heated more of the pole. All the while, he stared at it at his turned red, getting really hot really fast. When he seemed satisfied, he put the lighter into his pocket and examined the red-hot skinny, sharp pole, looking at Chloe with only his eyes, a grim smile on his face.

Chloe didn't have to question the situation. She knew *exactly* what was going to happen. She squirmed in her chair, pulling at the ropes on her hands, closing her eyes as the Gamer started to walk closer to her.

"Shhhh," he teased, putting his finger to her duct taped lips. Then, his hand slid down her neck until he was holding the neck of her shirt, ripping it down slightly to form a very low v-neck before he slowly brought the fire-heated pole toward her.

She squirmed more, squeezing her eyes shut, arms tense, knowing what pain was going to come, "Please!" She screamed, but the duct tape made the plea less affective.

He ignored her, as she expected, and brought the pole to her skin with a steady hand. As it touched her skin, the sizzle was audible, even through the deep, pained screams that were loud through the tape. She clenched her jaw, fingernails digging into the ropes that bound her wrists; she felt sweat run down her face as some blood ran down her chest from the "G" and the "A" as it was carved into her underneath her collarbone.

Kal was yelling through his tape, and though his words weren't understandable, the anger in them was clear as it could get.

As the Gamer began the "M", he smiled, eyes meeting Chloe's.

She stared back, fire and hate in her eyes as she gritted her teeth, a tear rolling down from her eye.

"Does it hurt?" He asked, sounding pleased.

She didn't respond; and that was a mistake.

He stood up straight and punched her as hard as he could in the face, knocking over the chair. Her face slammed into the ground, her arms not able to catch her. Finally, after letting her lay there for a while, he picked up the chair, setting it back up.

"Does it hurt?" He repeated, like nothing had ever happened, kneeling down again and continuing his brand.

She gritted her teeth, nodding.

"Good girl."

Blood was filling her mouth; and, unable to go anywhere else, it just kept filling from her busted lip. She had no choice, all she could do was swallow, which immediately made her gag. The Gamer, after finishing his "E", looked at her with a worried face at her gagging, then he took off the duct tape, blood spilling out of her mouth.

"Now, now," he said, "stop choking."

She spit blood onto his face.

This didn't seem to phase him, he just simply continued talking, "Hold still, I'm almost done. Wouldn't wanna screw it up now that it's over, would ya?"

Blood leaked down her chin as she cried slightly, tilting her head back, tears running down both cheeks as he touched the burning metal to her flesh again, slowly finishing the brand with an "R", causing her to scream again. The scream slowed into a whimper as he took away the metal and tossed it down onto the floor, standing up straight once again.

"Now," he clapped his hands together, looking from Chloe to Kal, "Time for the real fun."

"You're psychotic." Chloe spat out more blood as she talked.

He laughed to himself, digging into the box, looking over his shoulder to ask, "Who's first?"

"Fuck you." Chloe retorted, blood flowing down her mouth and chin as she glared at him, wishing and praying that he would fall over dead.

The Gamer stood up, smiling, a chainsaw in his right hand.

Chloe's brain froze as she looked blankly down at the chainsaw, "Are you shitting me?"

He pulled, trying to start the chainsaw.

Pulling on the ropes again to try to get free, Chloe looked over at Kal, who was rocking his body back and forth hard in the chair. The force knocked the chair over backwards and it crashed into a broken kitchen chair, wooden pieces clattering to the floor. As if it were his plan all along, Kal rolled out of the debris and tore off his duct tape, then used his teeth to tear off the ropes on his wrists.

Through it all, the Gamer was watching, and he looked impressed, but still bored as he started the chainsaw, which Chloe used to her advantage. The chainsaw was sitting there, on and tame, humming evenly as the Gamer watched Kal get up and out of his ropes, waiting to make his move. She leaned over, pushing her arms toward the roaring chainsaw, holding her breath at an attempt to keep her steady. After all, her life depended on it.

Kal stood, free of all ropes and duct tape, looking at the Gamer, stance challenging as he breathed triumphantly.

"I'll win, Kalvin!" The Gamer yelled over the chainsaw's loud growl.

Kal turned and opened a desk drawer, saying, "Not in this game," he pulled out a gun and cocked it, "You lose."

The Gamer's face changed rapidly: his smile was gone in two seconds flat, and for the first time, defeat was in his eyes.

Chloe, who freed herself with the chainsaw and had untied her legs, ran over to Kal, wiping her mouth with her ripped shirt, grabbing onto his arm as soon as she reached him.

"Are you okay?" He asked her as the roar of the chainsaw was silenced.

She nodded quickly, their attention quickly placed back onto the Gamer.

He looked extremely hostile, holding the gun tightly with both hands. Chloe didn't think she could ever recall him looking this crazy, so she contemplated with herself on her opinion about whether or not Kal would shoot him. They both wanted him to suffer.

She grabbed onto the gun before he had the chance, "Kal…give this to me."

Kal stared at the Gamer, anger shaking him, so Chloe used a little bit of force pulling on the gun.

"Kal," she convinced as she took the gun into her hands, "go call the police, okay?"

He slowly faded out of it, surrendering the gun to her, agreeing, "Yeah…." He took out his cell phone and stepped only a couple of steps away, closer to the stairs to get a better signal, not wanting to let Chloe and the Gamer out of sight. He wasn't going to leave her alone with him.

The Gamer, who seemed to be accepting defeat, threw the chainsaw onto the floor. But then, he smirked. Chloe's eyes narrowed cautiously as she watched him…. His hand moved quickly, grabbing a gun from his back pocket, but suddenly, Chloe shot the gun in her hand. She shot once, twice, three, four, five times. The Gamer's bloody, dead body fell to the floor, his gun limp in his hand.

"You lose," she threw the gun onto the floor.

CHAPTER 13
THE END

She looked at him in the same way she always had as he was driving them to school. It was considerably warmer, with less rain, the fresh new summer just around the corner. The truck windows were rolled down, and Kal's arm was lying on the open window, tapping it with one finger absentmindedly. He looked over at her, catching her in another one of her stares. She smiled and took his hand, biting her lip as she looked back up at him, watching his hair blow around in the wind.

They won.

The Gamer was dead.

It was all over.

They had won the Gamer's game.